Also by Lou Kuenzler

Princess Dis Grace First Term at Tall Towers
Princess Dis Grace Second Term at Tall Towers

SHRINKING VIOLET
SHRINKING VIOLET DEFINITELY NEEDS A DOG
SHRINKING VIOLET IS TOTALLY FAMOUS
SHRINKING VIOLET ABSOLUTELY LOVES ANCIENT EGYPT

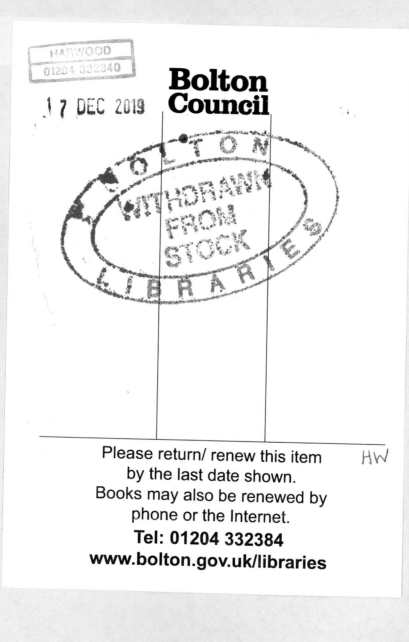

Bolton
Council

Please return/ renew this item
by the last date shown.
Books may also be renewed by
phone or the Internet.

HW

Tel: 01204 332384
www.bolton.gov.uk/libraries

Princess DisGrace

Third Term at Tall Towers

Lou Kuenzler
Illustrated by Kimberley Scott

A giant curtsy for all those who have helped with this book: brilliant editors Genevieve Herr and Emily Lamm at Scholastic, Rachel Phillipps for Publicity and all the Right-Royal rights and sales teams! Also Pat and Lexie at RCW, Sophie McKenzie and Julia Leonard for ongoing and ever brilliant advice. A big bow to my family too for letting me sneak away to my chamber to write.

First published in the UK in 2015 by Scholastic Children's Books
An imprint of Scholastic Ltd
Euston House, 24 Eversholt Street,
London, NW1 1DB, UK
Registered office: Westfield Road, Southam, Warwickshire, CV47 0RA
SCHOLASTIC and associated logos are trademarks and/or registered
trademarks of Scholastic Inc.

ISBN 978 1407 13630 1

A CIP catalogue record for this book
is available from the British Library.

Printed and bound by CPI Group (UK) Ltd, Croydon, CR0 4YY

Papers used by Scholastic Children's Books are made
from wood grown in sustainable forests.

3 5 7 9 10 8 6 4 2

www.scholastic.co.uk

To my girls as always
        -LK

CHAPTER ONE
An Exciting Announcement

Neat rows of golden chairs were arranged on the sunlit lawn where the royal pupils at Tall Towers Princess Academy were gathered for their first assembly of the summer term.

"Good Morning, Lady DuLac," chorused the princesses as everyone rose to their feet and curtsied to the headmistress in her long blue gown.

Princess Grace was so excited to be back for her third term at Tall Towers that she jumped up quickest of all. "Sorry!" she said,

nearly knocking over her two best friends, Princess Scarlet and Princess Izumi.

"Careful!" giggled the girls. They each grabbed an arm and steadied Grace before she toppled over completely.

"How pathetic! Look at Princess DisGrace," hissed a voice from the row of chairs behind. "She can't even do a proper curtsy yet."

Grace knew, without turning round, that it was her cousin Princess Precious who was talking. Like Grace, she was a First Year at Tall Towers.

"Oh, Precious, you are funny!" snorted the twin princesses, Trinket and Truffle. Grace would recognize their voices anywhere — they sounded like two snuffly piglets with their snouts in a trough. And they thought everything Precious said was...

"Absolutely hilarious!" as they both snorted now.

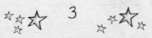

3

Grace had promised herself she would try and be more princessy this term. But she spun round and was just about to stick out her tongue at Precious when she caught sight of their strict form teacher, Fairy Godmother Flint, staring at her from the end of the row. Old Flintheart, as the girls called her, was dressed from head to foot in black robes and had a steely glare which could wilt the petals of a rose.

Grace almost bit off her tongue, she was so quick to pop it back in her mouth. She smiled innocently at Flintheart, trying to look as perfect, proper and princessy as she possibly could.

"Welcome back for another term at Tall Towers …" Lady DuLac was saying, as the princesses all sat down again on their little golden chairs.

"I wonder what news she'll have for us?" Grace whispered to Scarlet and Izumi, as Flintheart finally turned away.

"You never know what's going to happen next at Tall Towers," agreed Izumi. She was so tiny, compared with her tall, willowy friend, that she had to stretch right out of her chair to whisper into Grace's ear.

"As long as there are no more dragons on the island," gulped pretty, red-haired Princess Scarlet, leaning towards Grace from the other side.

"Poor Huffle!" Grace grinned, remembering the little red dragon she had secretly raised in a cave last term. "He really didn't mean anyone any harm."

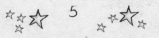

Scarlet raised her eyebrows and smiled.

"I'm going to sketch in the gardens, now it's summer," whispered artistic Izumi.

"I'm going to have a billion picnics and ride Billy flat out on the beach," grinned Grace, thinking of the fun she could have galloping her shaggy unicorn along the sand. She was about to suggest that the girls should slip down to the stables for a minute or two after assembly, when she heard Lady DuLac making an announcement.

"As soon as this assembly is over, all First Year princesses should return to the Dormitory Tower and get changed," she said.

"Changed?" murmured Grace. She wondered if they were supposed to put on their riding habits. Perhaps they'd get to see the unicorns after all. Or perhaps there was dance class and they'd have to change into their tutus.

"Now it is summer, you will begin your school swimming lessons," smiled Lady DuLac.

"Swimming! How perfect," whispered Grace, fidgeting as the hot morning sun beat down on her neck. "Who teaches us?" She couldn't imagine old Flintheart putting on a bathing suit and diving into the water. It would be like taking a vampire bat for a bath.

"Don't you remember?" said Scarlet, her eyes wide with surprise.

"At Tall Towers," announced Lady DuLac, "all princesses are taught to swim by mermaids."

"Mermaids? Whoopee!" Grace leapt right out of her chair and cheered. It was just about the most exciting thing she could imagine. Scarlet was right; she had heard about the mermaid teachers before, but she had never quite believed it was true.

"Princess Grace, sit down this instant!" hissed Flintheart.

"Sorry." Grace flopped back on to her chair, but even Flintheart's furious stare couldn't stop her grinning from ear to ear.

"I think Princess Grace has expressed what we all feel," smiled Lady DuLac kindly. "We are very lucky to have mermaids visiting our school."

Grace turned to look at her friends.

Sure enough, Izumi was beaming. The other First Years were grinning too. All except Scarlet. She looked terrified.

"Oh dear, I've never learnt to swim," she said. Her big sea-green eyes were flashing with fear.

CHAPTER TWO
Clamshell Cove

"Hurry up, girls!" Grace grabbed her towel and dashed to the door of Sky Dorm, the little attic bedroom she shared with Scarlet and Izumi.

"Careful!" cried Scarlet.

"Look out!" said Izumi.

But it was too late. Grace was running so fast she tripped over the end of the trailing towel and landed in a tangle on the floor. "Oops!" she giggled. "I don't want to twist my ankle before we even meet the mermaids." She felt a fizz of excitement in her tummy.

"I wish we had a little more time to settle back in before the swimming lessons begin," said Scarlet. Her hands were shaking as she brushed her long red hair. "I'm the only princess in the class who can't swim at all."

"I wouldn't worry. I just flop about like a seal," grinned Grace. She thought of the freezing grey lake where her father had taught her to swim at home – the trick was to splash as much as possible or your fingers and toes turned to ice. It would be wonderful to float calmly here in the sunny blue waters of Clamshell Cove.

"The mermaids are going to teach us how to swim gracefully," she said. "You'll be brilliant at that, Scarlet – you're such a wonderful dancer."

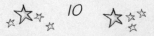

Scarlet smiled shyly. She was the best ballerina in the whole class.

"Come on," cried Grace, tying a knot in the end of her frizzy brown plaits. "Last one in the water's a jellyfish." She thundered down the twisting stairs of the Dormitory Tower. "Whoops!" she squealed, almost colliding with Princess Latisha as she came out of Sea Dorm on the floor below.

Latisha, who was very sporty, looked just about as excited as Grace. "I wonder if we'll have swimming races," she grinned as she sprinted down the stairs.

"I hope I'm on your team if we do," panted Grace, trying to keep up.

"Me too," said Izumi, following behind.

It was only as Grace tumbled down the very last step that she realized Scarlet wasn't with them. "You go on," she said to the others. "I'll wait for her."

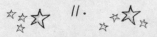

"Are you sure?" asked Izumi.

Grace nodded. She was desperate to see the mermaids for herself, but she knew how nervous poor Scarlet was feeling.

"See you in a minute," smiled Izumi, following Latisha as they headed towards the cliff path. "Don't forget ... last one in the pool is a jellyfish! You said so yourself."

"Flubber-dubber!" laughed Grace, shaking her arms and legs as if she was an enormous jelly creature.

"Help!" Izumi pretended to be terrified and dashed away.

"COME ON, SCARLET!" Grace bellowed, hollering up the long staircase and dancing excitedly from foot to foot. It felt so good to be back at school with her friends again.

"What is that horrible noise?" said a sharp voice. The door to Fairy Godmother Flint's ground-floor office opened with a *whoosh*

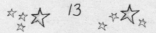

13

and Flintheart poked her long thin nose out into the hall. "Princess Grace," she sighed. "I might have known it was you making that horrible, un-princess-like hullabaloo."

"Sorry." Grace gave a wobbly curtsy, desperate not to be in trouble again when the new term had hardly even begun. She was out of practice after the long holiday and her curtsy was worse than usual – she almost stepped on her form teacher's toe.

"Just because you are going to the beach for a swimming lesson," sighed the fairy godmother, "does not mean that you need to honk like a squawking seagull. A proper princess never raises her voice, remember?"

"Yes, Fairy Godmother," blushed Grace.

She had forgotten just how hard it was to be a proper princess. And Fairy Godmother Flint always seemed to think that she ought to try a lot harder still.

"Hurry along," said the form teacher firmly as Scarlet appeared on the stairs looking pearly white with fear.

Grace squeezed her friend's hand as they hurried towards the sea. "Don't worry. It'll be like it was when we first rode our unicorns," she said. "Remember how scared you were to even sit on Velvet before you had a proper lesson? Now you gallop all over Coronet Island."

"That's true," said Scarlet. "But the water has always frightened me."

"It does go up your nose a bit if you breathe in at the wrong time," laughed Grace. "But I bet the mermaids will have you diving for coral in no time."

"Not on our first lesson, I hope?" shivered Scarlet.

Grace was trying to make her friend feel better but realized she was probably making

★☆ *15* ☆

things worse. Yet, a moment later, even Scarlet smiled as they wound their way down the steep cliff path and caught a glimpse of the sheltered swimming cove below. The deep, natural rock pool was a perfect shell shape. There wasn't a single wave on the bright, clear surface, glistening bright turquoise in the sun.

"Wow!" Grace gasped. Although she had seen the pool before, it had never looked quite as magical as it did today. Perhaps it was knowing that the mermaids must be somewhere near.

She had only ever glimpsed a real mermaid once before – just the flash of a tail from a boat. The icy waters at home were far too chilly for merfolk to stay around long. But the sea here, on the shores of Coronet Island, looked as warm and clear as the cloudless, blue sky above.

"It really is beautiful," whispered Scarlet.

The whole class had gathered on the edge of the sand in an excited gaggle.

Only Precious didn't seem impressed. "Mummy says I don't have to swim if I don't want to," she said, flicking her long golden hair. "The seawater might ruin my curls."

Grace opened and closed her mouth like a goldfish. She could understand Scarlet hanging back because she was afraid, but was Precious really going to refuse to go in the water just because of her hair?

"I want to try and dive for shells," said Latisha. "My older sister says the deep end drops down further than a well."

"I couldn't care less about silly shells ... or mermaids," said Precious. "The only good thing ever to come out of the sea was these pearls." She raised her hand to her throat and clutched at the valuable necklace she always wore.

"We're not meant to wear jewellery in the pool in case it gets lost," said Scarlet, looking worried. "I left my silver locket in the dormitory."

"I can do what I want," said Precious. "It's my necklace. It's been in my family

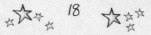

for generations, since the time of my Great-Grandmother Joy."

"*Our* Great-Grandmother Joy," said Grace with a cheeky grin. She knew that Precious hated being reminded she was related to someone from such a tiny, scruffy little kingdom as Grace. But, because they were

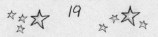

cousins, they shared the same grandparents –
and great-grandparents, of course – on their
mothers' side of the family.

"You're just jealous, Grace," snapped
Precious. "One of these tiny pearls is probably
worth more than your whole grotty little
kingdom."

"I'm not jealous at all," said Grace,
truthfully. She never really wore jewellery
in case she broke it or lost it somewhere.
She certainly wouldn't trust herself with the
treasured family pearls. "I'd rather have a
yummy box of chocolates than a big shiny
jewel any day," she grinned.

"Good for you, Grace," laughed wealthy
Princess Visalotta. She was the richest
princess in the class – in the whole *world*,
some people said. But, unlike Precious, she
never judged anyone for how big or small
their kingdom was.

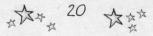

She linked arms with Grace and pointed to the shimmering turquoise pool. "Even a mountain of jewels couldn't buy anything as beautiful as that," she said.

"Look!" Grace saw a splash on the surface of the water and a flash of emerald green. She felt her heart leap like a flying fish. "I think that was a mermaid's tail," she gasped.

CHAPTER THREE
Swimming With Mermaids

The First Years jostled forward. Grace was sure it was a tail she had seen flickering in the water.

A moment later, the dark head of a beautiful black-haired woman rose up from the surface of the pool. Her skin was as smooth and bronzed as driftwood on a beach. As she slithered on to the rocks, the girls saw she had a sparkling, green tail, which gleamed in the sunlight.

"Greetings, Young Majesties. My name is

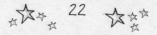

Oceana," she said, her voice rising and falling like waves.

A second, much younger, mermaid appeared beside her. She was a beautiful teenager, who didn't look much older than the Sixth Form princesses at Tall Towers. Her skin was as pale as Precious's string of pearls and her blonde hair tumbled to her waist. "I'm Waverley," she said softly.

"Look!" whispered Princess Truffle, one of the twins. "Her curls are twice as thick as yours, Precious."

"Shut up, Truffle," hissed Precious. "Nobody cares what you think."

"Yes, shut up, Truffle," giggled Princess Trinket, the other twin.

Waverley slid on to the rocks. The young mermaid's tail was silver and shone like a million diamonds.

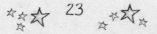 23

"I don't see what all the fuss is about," mumbled Precious. "They're just fancy fish."

Grace raised her eyebrows. Trust Precious to be jealous just because Waverley's hair was longer and thicker than hers. She could say what she liked, but the mermaids were beautiful. Far lovelier than the pictures Grace had seen in the fairy-tale books her little sister, Princess Pip, loved to read.

"Welcome, dear mermaids," said Lady DuLac, who had come down to the beach too. She bowed to the mermaids. "I have looked forward to your visit for many months."

"Thank you, Headmistress. I am always excited to teach your youngest princesses," said Oceana. "And this is the first time Waverley has come to the school to help me." She beckoned the young mermaid

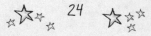

forward and Waverley began to sing, as if in greeting, to the headmistress and her Tall Towers pupils.

A long clear, tingling note echoed across the pool. The sound was more like a musical instrument than a song – it seemed to Grace to catch all the sadness and mystery of the sea.

"Gosh, how can she sing so high?" gasped musical Princess Martine, who had a beautiful voice of her own.

Grace wasn't at all musical – when she sang, it sounded as if a frog was trying to clear its throat – but even she could tell the young mermaid's voice was as fine as any flute or violin could ever hope to be. The singing made Grace feel as if she wanted to dive to the bottom of the deepest ocean and swim along the seabed amongst coral and starfish.

"Do you feel it too?" whispered Scarlet, gripping her hand. "Like they're calling you to the sea?"

"It's probably some kind of enchantment," huffed Precious as Waverley tossed her hair. The mermaid's curls shimmered like a waterfall of spun gold. "Merfolk are always casting spells on people. I don't think they should be allowed to come anywhere near the school."

"What nonsense," said Grace. "If there is any magic, it comes from the mystery of the sea. I think it's exciting."

"You may get into the water," said Oceana, motioning the princesses forward.

Grace couldn't wait a moment longer. She tossed her towel onto the rocks, let out a whoop of joy and dive-bombed into the sparkling, blue pool.

A huge splash rose up around her like a swirling skirt of water.

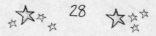

"Yippee!" she cheered. The sea was as warm as a bath.

As Grace rolled on to her back, she saw that the other princesses were stepping gently down the sunken steps, edging into the water like graceful swans.

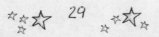

"I suppose it would have been more princessy to do it like that," she giggled.

Scarlet was still standing nervously on the side. Grace swam back towards her.

The twins, meanwhile, had managed to encourage Precious on to the steps.

"I suppose I might come in," she said, wrinkling her nose and dipping a toe in the water as if it was a puddle of mud rather than a sparkling sapphire pool. "After all, it's not like I'm scared or anything." Precious shot a mean look at Scarlet and burst into fits of giggles.

"That's enough!" said Grace, pounding towards the shallow end. She had a good mind to dunk Precious's curly gold head right under the water.

But Oceana swam between them. "You need to remove your necklace before you get in the water," she said, as Precious teetered on the steps.

Precious blew out her cheeks and pouted.

"You don't want to lose it amongst the rocks at the bottom of the pool," said Visalotta. Grace noticed that the wealthy princess had taken off her own gold and silver bracelets and the ruby necklace and emerald earrings she often wore – as well as her diamond tiara, of course.

"I never let this necklace out of my sight," said Precious sulkily. She looked round the pool with narrowed eyes as if she thought the mermaids might want to steal it.

"I'll look after it for you," said Scarlet, stretching out her hand.

"But aren't you coming in?" said Grace.

"I–I don't feel very well," said Scarlet.

"But..." began Grace. She knew Scarlet was just scared. She'd feel much better once she got in the water. If she stayed

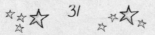

in the shallow end, near the steps, her feet would never need to leave the bottom. "The mermaids will help you if you tell them you've never had a swimming lesson before," she said, just loud enough so that only Scarlet could hear her.

But Scarlet looked away as if she hadn't heard a thing. "I really don't feel well, Lady DuLac," she said, pleading with the headmistress, who was still close to the pool. "If I sit out I can look after Precious's necklace so it won't come to any harm."

"I suppose there's some truth in that," said Lady DuLac kindly. Grace was certain the headmistress could see how afraid Scarlet was. "From now on, I suggest you all leave your jewellery safely in the dormitories when you get changed." She looked pointedly at Precious, before bowing to the mermaids and turning towards school.

Precious stuck out her bottom lip. "I never take my pearls off," she whined. "I don't even think they come unclipped."

"Let me help you," said Oceana, sliding through the water like a dolphin.

"I can do it myself!" Precious leapt backwards. "Keep your fins away from me," she muttered under her breath.

"I beg your pardon?" Lady DuLac spun round. She had obviously heard every word. "You will kindly remember you are addressing a teacher, Princess Precious. Show some respect."

The headmistress did not raise her voice. She never did. But Grace watched her cousin blush with shame. A quiet word of warning from Lady DuLac was far more terrible than a furious telling-off from Fairy Godmother Flint or any of the other teachers. Every princess in the school wanted to please the silver-haired headmistress and make her proud.

"Here!" Precious almost threw the necklace at Scarlet as Lady DuLac carried on towards the cliffs. "Just wait until my mummy hears about this!"

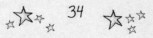

What a lot of fuss over a necklace, thought Grace, rolling on to her tummy and splashing Precious just a little more than she meant to as she kicked her feet and paddled away to the other end of the pool.

CHAPTER FOUR
The Pearls

Grace swam up and down the pool with the other princesses as the mermaids called out encouragement.

"Today we just want to see how well you can swim," said Oceana. "Tomorrow we will teach you to move through the water like elegant sea nymphs..."

"Yikes!" said Grace, swallowing a mouthful of salty water. She wasn't certain exactly what a sea nymph was, but she was sure swimming like one would be a

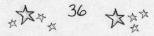

lot harder than the scissor legs she was practising now.

"You're doing very well, Princess Grace," said Oceana, gliding past with a flick of her tail. "Perhaps don't kick *quite* so hard though."

Grace glanced over her shoulder and saw that she had drenched poor Scarlet. She was sitting on the rocks beside the deep end of the pool, looking after Precious's pearls as she had promised.

"Sorry!" Grace floundered over and grabbed Scarlet's towel from the side of the pool. "Dry yourself with this."

"Careful! The pearls!" warned Scarlet.

But it was too late. As Grace snatched the towel, Precious's necklace splashed into the water.

"Quick – catch it!" cried Grace, fighting desperately to free her hands from the towel,

which was wrapped around her like a damp octopus.

Instantly Scarlet dived forward, bravely throwing herself into the water.

"Wait!" gasped Grace as Scarlet disappeared under the surface to catch the sinking necklace. "It's too deep for you here!"

Grace looked round in panic. She knew that Scarlet couldn't swim. Waverley was racing Latisha flat out on the far side of the pool. All the other princesses were gathered in the shallow end, splashing their legs as Oceana clapped a rhythm for them to kick to. Grace opened her mouth to scream for help – but stopped, frozen in surprise. Beneath the clear blue surface, Scarlet was diving straight as an arrow – swimming down, down, down towards the deep bottom of the pool.

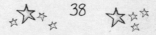

Grace clung to the side of the rocks, the panic turning to pride inside her. *I should have known,* she smiled to herself. Scarlet was a brilliant swimmer even though she had never been in the water before. She was as graceful and elegant in the sea as she was on the dance floor.

"Amazing!" cheered Grace, and then, realizing Scarlet wouldn't be able to hear her, she flung the wet towel on the side of the pool and dived down to help her friend find the pearls.

As soon as Grace's head was below the water, the noise and splashing of the swimming lesson disappeared. Ahead, she could see Scarlet's pale legs kicking through the water — it was as if they were all alone down here in an ocean world.

Grace held her breath as she reached a broad ledge of rock about halfway down the side of the pool. Perhaps the pearls had landed here. She was already desperate to bob back to the surface and gasp for air. Scarlet had been under the water even longer but was still swimming straight and low, her knees and ankles tight together, her legs rippling like a fish's tail.

Grace blinked in the shadowy water, hoping to see a flash of white from the pearls. Her fingers searched the rocky ledge, finding only tiny pebbles and shells. She glanced down, on towards the darkness at

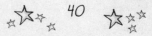

the bottom of the pool. Scarlet was still diving – how deep would she swim? Grace tried to follow but she felt as if a balloon was going to burst inside her chest. She couldn't stay under a moment longer.

"Phew!" With a great gulping gasp, she broke back through the surface and clung spluttering to the rocks around the edge of the pool.

Izumi saw her and swam over. "Are you all right?" she asked, patting Grace's back.

Grace nodded. "Scarlet's still down there," she said. "She dived in to save Precious's pearls."

"But how. . .? She's never had swimming lessons." Izumi peered at the shimmering water as Scarlet's shadow flickered beneath them for a second.

"That's amazing," said Princess Latisha, who had swum up alongside the two friends. "I've never seen anyone swim like that."

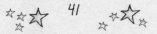

Grace stared downwards but Scarlet had vanished in the darkness again. "She's been down there too long," she said, holding her breath and getting ready to dive once more.

"Oceana! Waverley!" called Izumi. "We need help. Come quick."

But a second later Scarlet burst through the surface of the pool, her long red hair dripping wet. She raised her arm and held the pearls high above her head. "Got them," she said as she scrambled to the side of the pool and collapsed on the rocks in a shivering heap.

"You were brilliant!" cheered Grace, rubbing Scarlet's legs with a towel – before she realized it was the sopping-wet one she had dropped in the water.

"Here." Izumi found a dry towel and wrapped it around Scarlet as she sat up with her shoulders hunched.

"Are you all right, Young Majesty?" asked Waverley.

Scarlet nodded. Her lips were trembling.

"That looked like some pretty good swimming," said the mermaid with a smile.

"What's going on?" asked Precious, doggy-paddling over with her head high out of the water so that her hair wouldn't get wet. She looked like a fluffy golden poodle that had accidentally fallen into a bath. "Has Grace pushed Scarlet in, or something?"

"Actually, Scarlet saved your necklace," said Grace. "It – er – dropped to the bottom of the pool."

"My pearls?" shrieked Precious. "I bet that was your fault, Grace. You're such a clumsy oaf..."

"Clumsy oaf," echoed the twins.

"It was an accident," said Grace, a little shakily. Her heart was still pounding. Scarlet had taken a terrible risk ... but imagine if the pearls had been lost for ever.

"It wasn't Grace's fault," said Scarlet, staring at the pearls as if she couldn't take

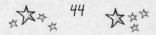

her eyes off them. "I put the necklace down. I should have kept hold of it like I promised."

"I'll never trust you again. Either of you!" said Precious, snatching the necklace from Scarlet's shaking fingers. She paddled away in a huff with the twins splashing behind her, honking in sympathy like two sea lions.

"Phew, that was a close one!" Grace flung her wet arms around her friend. "I think Precious would have tried to drown us both if the pearls had sunk."

Scarlet smiled weakly.

"You were amazing in the water. I couldn't even see what I was doing and you went so much deeper than me," said Grace. "How did you hold your breath for so long? It was as if you were a real mermaid."

"Don't." Scarlet shot her a look of panic. "It was horrible being under water," she said

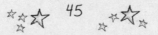 45

as she staggered to her feet. She grabbed the dry towel Izumi had given her and sprinted away across the beach. "I'm going back to Tall Towers."

"Wait," called Oceana. "The lesson is not over yet."

But Scarlet kept on running.

Grace watched her scrambling up the steep cliff path. Halfway up she passed Lady DuLac, who held out her hand as if urging Scarlet to stop. But the princess dodged sideways and hurtled on.

Grace had never seen her friend ignore a teacher before — especially not the headmistress herself. Scarlet was tripping and falling as she ran, looking more like Grace with her shoelaces undone than the elegant ballerina she really was.

"I don't understand," said Izumi, clambering out of the pool too. "Scarlet

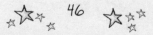

should be proud of the way she dived in like that."

"She's a natural," agreed Princess Latisha.

Grace frowned. It was true. Scarlet had proved she was a wonderful swimmer. So why was she so upset? Was it just the shock? Or had something happened down there?

CHAPTER FIVE
Birthday Plans

With all the excitement of meeting the mermaids and settling back into school, Grace had almost forgotten that it was her birthday at the end of the week.

"You're so lucky," said Izumi, holding the gate for Grace and Scarlet as they rode their unicorns out of the stable yard one sunny afternoon. "You've got your special Tall Towers birthday tea to look forward to."

"We can all get dressed in our fanciest clothes," grinned Scarlet, seeming more

relaxed than she had for days. She had refused to go anywhere near the pool since she'd dived for the pearls, making a different excuse every time there was a swimming lesson. First she said she was ill. Then she pretended she couldn't find her costume – although Grace had seen her stuff it under her bed. This morning, she claimed she'd misread her timetable and gone to the dance studio instead. Scarlet *never* made mistakes like that. She was the most organized person Grace knew. Something was definitely wrong. But at least she had cheered up at the thought of a party.

"I hope there'll be a big wobbly jelly, bubbly lemonade and LOTS of chocolate," smiled Grace.

"Ooh, and heart-shaped sandwiches... And those little butterfly biscuits too," said Izumi.

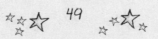 49

It was a Tall Towers tradition that whenever a princess had a birthday during term time, an enormous cake and plates of party food were laid out for her to share with her classmates in the beautiful marble ballroom beneath the crystal chandeliers.

There was dancing and party games too. It was all very different from home, where Grace's birthday parties had usually involved roast yak on a spit, a tug-of-war with her father's warriors and Jape the jester giving her the bumps – which meant throwing her up in the air, higher and higher for every year of her life. A Tall Towers birthday celebration certainly sounded a lot more proper for a princess.

"I do wish we could have the party in the stables though," said Grace. "Think what fun it would be to have tea with the unicorns."

"You are impossible," laughed Izumi. "You know Billy would only eat all the cake."

"That's true," said Grace, leaning forward to scratch her scruffy black-and-white unicorn between the ears.

Billy was the greediest unicorn in the whole school. He turned his head now,

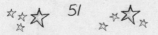

hoping she might have a handful of pomegranate seeds for him.

"It's time you had a good gallop," said Grace firmly. They'd spent so much time in the swimming pool with the mermaids, this was the first chance she'd had to give Billy a really good ride. "Let's go down to the beach," said Grace, pulling Billy's reins to the left. The long, flat sand was one of her favourite places to gallop.

"Great idea," said Izumi, turning Beauty, her unicorn, in the same direction.

"I'm not sure," said Scarlet. "I'd rather go up to the moors." But her pretty dapple-grey unicorn, Velvet, had other ideas.

As soon as the three unicorns saw the sandy path that led to the beach, their ears pricked with excitement. Billy was off like a cannonball.

"It'll be brilliant, Scarlet," cried Grace over

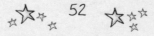

her shoulder. "You know how Velvet loves to gallop in the waves."

But when they reached the beach, Scarlet kept Velvet on a tight rein, close to the dry sand on the dunes. Izumi and Grace let their unicorns gallop in the edge of the surf – splashing up water as they thundered along. Their legs and arms and even their faces were soaked with spray.

Grace was surprised Scarlet didn't join in the fun. "Come on down," she cried, blinking as she tried to see through the shower of seawater. Her voice must have been carried away on the wind because Scarlet didn't seem to hear. She stayed up on the powdery, dry sand far away from the shore.

"Steady!" said Izumi as they reached the end of the beach and Beauty slowed to a gentle trot.

"Whoa!" Billy swerved sideways. He

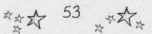

spotted a tasty strand of green seaweed and skidded to a stop so fast that Grace flew right over his head and landed in the edge of the sea. A wave splashed down the back of her neck. "I should have worn my swimming costume," she laughed, grabbing Billy's reins and squelching to the side of a rock pool to empty the water from her boots.

"You do look soggy," laughed Izumi.

Although it was late afternoon, the sun was still bright and warm. Grace clambered out of her soaking-wet riding clothes so that she was wearing just her vest and knickers. "I'll lay everything out on the rocks to dry for a bit," she said, flapping her socks in the wind. "Is it all right if we let the unicorns graze at the edge of the dunes for a while?"

"Fine by me," said Izumi, loosening Beauty's girth. "We can play the shell game while we wait."

 54

"Yes, let's," said Scarlet, her lovely broad smile back again at last.

Artistic Izumi loved to search the rocks and sand for pretty shells until she found her favourite. This long stretch of sandy beach had brilliant specimens and was one of the best places on the island to play the game. "Ten minutes, then," she said. "And we'll meet back here at the rock pool with our favourite shells."

"I'll stay near the unicorns," said Scarlet, heading up to the dry dunes again. "Someone ought to watch them."

Izumi already had her head bent low, walking right up the middle of the beach.

Grace dashed down to the sea again. Now her legs were bare, it wouldn't matter if she got wet. "We can swap over in a while if you like," she called to Scarlet.

But Scarlet shook her head.

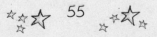 55

★

Ten minutes later they all met back at the shallow rock pool. Izumi was carrying her boots now too, and she and Grace washed their sandy feet.

"Ready?" said Izumi, holding out her hand, which was closed in a tight fist. "After three, show your shells."

"One . . ." counted Grace, holding out her tightly closed hand.

"Two . . ." Scarlet joined in.

"Three!" said Izumi and the girls opened their hands to reveal their shells.

Izumi's a was tiny scallop-shaped one, with streaks of bright colour almost as if the marks had been made by a paintbrush. Scarlet's was a pale white curling spiral. The circles twisted in towards the centre, growing ever tighter, like a ballerina spinning in a pirouette.

"Amazing! The shells you've picked suit

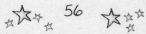

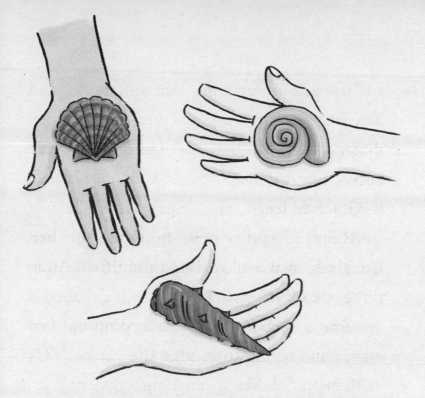

you both so perfectly," said Grace, thinking
how well the two different shapes matched
her friends' artistic and graceful personalities.

"And yours is just like you," said Izumi.

"It is!" giggled Scarlet.

Grace looked down at the thin, knobbly
shell she had chosen. It had spikes poking
out in every direction. "How is this like
me?" she asked.

"It's sort of exciting and different," said Scarlet.

"A little wild," laughed Izumi. "But very pretty."

Grace blushed. She didn't think she was anything like the delicate shell but was delighted that her friends thought she was.

"Look at Mermaid Rock — it's shaped a bit like a shell too," she said, pointing out to sea and trying to change the subject. "Or perhaps more like a sea king's trident."

The distant silvery rock rose above the waves in three tall spikes, each pointing up to the cloudless sky.

"It's supposed to be hollow inside," said Izumi. "A mermaid grotto, decorated with mother-of-pearl."

"I wonder if anyone ever gets to visit?" said Grace. The faraway rock seemed to glow, almost as if there was some sort of magic hidden inside.

"It is beautiful," said Scarlet. But Grace saw her friend shiver as she turned hurriedly away and ran up to the dunes to catch Velvet.

Izumi caught her unicorn too. "It's getting late. We ought to be heading back to school," she said.

"Coming," said Grace, scrambling into her dry clothes as Billy trotted to the edge of the waves to meet her. She put her foot in the stirrup and glanced out to sea one

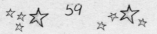

last time. It was odd... She felt a shiver run down her spine – as if the shimmering shadow of Mermaid Rock was sending its magic out across the waves towards them. Grace couldn't help feeling they were going to know more about the strange silvery rock before the summer term was over.

CHAPTER SIX
The Middle of the Night

Grace rolled over in her sleep.

Thud!

"Not again!" she groaned, opening one eye and realizing she had fallen out of bed. The same thing happened every night. Usually, Grace didn't wake up until morning when she would find herself curled up on the dormitory floor, her long legs tucked inside her nightie. But there was no way she was going to get back to sleep tonight. She'd been dreaming about her party – her

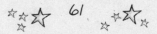

tummy was zinging with excitement like popping candy on a cupcake.

"Anyone awake?" she whispered, wishing she could tell her friends how the birthday cake in her dream had been so tall that Billy had grown wings like a Pegasus pony and flown up to the very top to nibble the chocolate icing. In her dream, the mermaids had been at the party too, sitting with their tails curled around the legs of shiny gold chairs. The floor of the great hall was flooded with seawater so that everybody else had to wear wellington boots.

"Izumi?" Grace whispered, feeling like she might pop with excitement. But Izumi's dark head was motionless on her pillow, her lips parted slightly as she breathed in and out, deep in sleep.

"Scarlet?" Grace peeked into the other little white bed and nearly jumped out of her skin. It was empty.

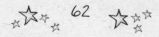

It wasn't like Scarlet to get up and go wandering about in the middle of night. It was strictly against the rules.

She's probably just gone to the loo, thought Grace, telling herself not to be silly. She forced herself to count slowly to a hundred under her breath and wait for Scarlet to come back.

"One unicorn horn ... two unicorn horns ... three unicorn horns..."

Grace only made it to ten before she jumped to her feet. She couldn't stand it a moment longer. She had to know where Scarlet had gone. She pulled on the ragged old pair of yak-fur slippers she had brought from home and grabbed her dressing gown.

Izumi stirred, but Grace couldn't bear to wake her up. She looked so peaceful. At least the fluffy slippers made Grace's footsteps quieter than usual. She slid through the door and tried to close it silently behind her.

HEEEEEEEEE! The hinge squeaked like a laughing witch. It never seemed to make so much noise in the daytime.

As soon as she was in the corridor, Grace poked her head into the bathroom. It was empty. No sign of Scarlet anywhere.

She stood at the top of the stairs for

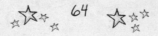

a moment, listening to the sounds of the sleeping Dormitory Tower. Suddenly, there was a creaking noise and a muffled bang from somewhere far below – another door was being opened and closed. This wasn't a high, whining squeak like the door to Sky Dorm though. This was a juddering sound like a heavy log being dragged across a stone floor.

The Great West Door, thought Grace. Someone must have gone out through the huge entrance at the bottom of the stairs. Surely Scarlet would never dare to step outside alone at night? It was breaking just about every school rule there was ... not to mention that there were bats and owls and the shadows of the dark trees in the garden.

Grace had to find out what was going on. She leapt down the stairs three at a time, slipping and sliding in her floppy slippers.

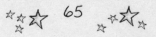

As she reached the last two floors of the high tower, she scrambled on to the banisters and slid down that way – twice as quickly as she could have run.

"Ouch!" Grace tripped over the doormat, fell through the open door and landed in a heap outside.

It was lighter in the garden than Grace had expected. Looking up she saw that the moon was nearly full. It was the shape of a big white egg – almost a perfect circle but not quite. Silvery moonlight flooded the grounds, throwing strange shadows on the statues and fountains.

"Scarlet, is that you?" Grace hissed, catching sight of a tall, flickering figure disappearing through a gateway at the end of the path. "Wait for me!"

Grace leapt to her feet but the figure ducked behind a wall and vanished.

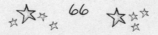

"Where are you going?" called Grace, but the only answer was the hooting of an owl. "Yikes!" She jumped as the snowy bird swooped low over her head. She glanced back towards the tower, hoping she hadn't woken anyone inside. She was desperate to know where Scarlet was going, but she didn't want to get her in trouble with Flintheart. If Scarlet was breaking the rules, she must have a very good reason. Normally, she wouldn't even return a library book late without worrying about being in trouble.

Grace waited a moment, looking back at the tower to check that no one else had woken up. Then she tightened her dressing-gown cord and ran across the lawn. She was the only person who even knew that Scarlet was outside. Anything could happen out here in the middle of the night.

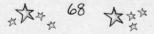

The owl flapped its wings, settling in a nearby tree.

Grace dashed on, following the pale figure towards the trees.

CHAPTER SEVEN
The Rescue

"Wait!" Grace lunged forward as she caught sight of the figure again on the path ahead. They were far enough away from school now that she could shout as loudly as she liked. "Scarlet, stop!" she hollered, certain that it was her friend. She would recognize that light, floating step anywhere. But why wouldn't she listen?

The figure kept moving, darting through the trees, heading in the direction of the beach. Grace dashed on along the winding

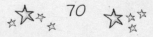

path behind her, desperate not to let Scarlet out of her sight. It wasn't easy to keep up. Her old, baggy slippers flopped like furry bear paws as she ran. They were large enough to fit her father's warriors and were at least three sizes too big even for Grace's enormous feet.

She reached the sand. As the moon flickered on the waves, Grace could see that the tide was coming in. She felt her heart thump. It wasn't safe to be near the water.

Quite suddenly, everything went dark. The sky above her was velvet black. The moon had disappeared into the clouds.

"Scarlet!" she called. "Come back to the path."

Grace turned, hoping she could still see a light burning in one of the towers at school. But it was too far away and everything was pitch black.

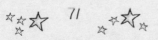

"Help!" she cried, wishing she hadn't been so foolish as to follow Scarlet all alone. She should have fetched help right away ... but it was too late now.

She could hear the suck and pull of the waves close by.

Suddenly Scarlet's voice cut through the darkness. "Grace! Is that you? It's me, Scarlet. I'm safe. I'm on the path."

"Thank goodness!" Grace began to run back through the gloom. "Stay where you are – I'm coming," she called.

But the sand was uneven and lumpy. "Whoops!" She tripped over her floppy feet and fell. She tried to scramble up but her slippers had filled with sand.

Whoosh! A wave drenched her from behind. The tide was coming in fast. Grace staggered to her feet, but her slippers filled with water as if they were two big buckets.

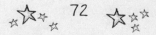

The sand inside them turned heavy and like wet cement.

"Grace?" called Scarlet. "Where are you?"

"I'm here." She tried to run but it was as if her feet were stuck in glue. Water was swooshing around her ankles, then her waist. "Urg!" She kicked desperately, freeing herself from the slippers at last. The water was cold and inky black. She tried to swim, paddling hard with her arms, but the waves were too strong and her mouth filled with salty water.

She was spinning, turning over and over in the waves – she didn't know which way was up and which way was down.

"Relax. I've got you!" said a soft voice. Grace felt a pair of strong arms grip her waist. She was dragged back towards the shore.

The clouds parted a little, at last, and pale moonlight shone through.

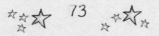 73

Grace tilted her head out of the water, trying to see who her rescuer was. She was sure it must be Scarlet, her long hair flowing around them as she pulled Grace towards safety. She remembered how well her friend had swum the day she dived for the pearls.

But then there was a splash in the water and Grace saw the silvery shimmer of a mermaid's tail...

How could that be?

"Scarlet?" she gasped.

"No!" said the gentle voice. "Scarlet is safe on the shore."

As Grace stumbled out of the waves and collapsed on the sand, she saw that her rescuer was Waverley, the young mermaid teacher.

"Thank you," breathed Grace. "You saved my life."

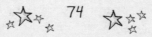

CHAPTER EIGHT
The Mermaid Code

Grace leapt up and dashed along the moonlit shore, water flying from the ends of her plaits and her wet nightie flapping round her knees as she ran. Her bare feet sank into the damp sand. She had lost her dressing gown and her slippers were somewhere far out at sea. "Scarlet," she cried, throwing her arms around her friend's neck. "I was so worried about you."

"Thank goodness you're safe," said Scarlet. "But I don't understand what I'm doing

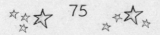

here? Why on earth did I come to the beach in the middle of the night?"

"I don't know," said Grace as they sat down on a rock. She was relieved to see Scarlet acting normally, even if she was still confused. "I followed you from the dormitory. I kept calling out but you didn't seem to hear me. You wouldn't stop."

"But it's against the rules to be out of bed after lights out," said Scarlet, blinking in horror.

Grace laughed. She couldn't help it. "Trust you to worry about the rules, Scarlet! You could have died of cold ... or drowned..." She threw her arms around Scarlet's neck again, before she realized she was making her poor friend soaking wet.

"I put us both in terrible danger," said Scarlet. "All I remember is sitting up in bed and feeling as if the sea was calling

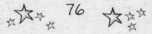

to me. Moonlight was streaming through the window. The next thing I knew, I was here. The moon disappeared and you were shouting to me from the waves."

"Perhaps you were sleepwalking," suggested Grace. "Pip did that once. We found her curled up with the yaks in the barn."

"Do you think that is all it was?" said Scarlet. Her face lit up with relief. But she jumped a little as Waverley swam up to the edge of the rocks beside them.

"Some people are drawn to the sea," said the mermaid. "They hear the waves talking to them. Calling their name. Especially if it is near the time of a full moon. It is the moon that controls the tides, you know. Did you feel something like that tonight?"

"I—I think so. I don't know." Scarlet looked confused again. She turned towards Grace, who was shivering now as water dripped from her soaking-wet nightie and made a pool around her feet. "Goodness. We should get you back to school," cried Scarlet. "You need to get warm and dry. Come on." She leapt to her feet.

Grace smiled. Scarlet was definitely her old self again, worrying about her friend. Grace's

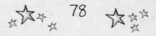

teeth were chattering like castanets and her knees were knocking together. It probably was time to go back to school – not to mention that Flintheart would be up soon.

Scarlet ran on ahead. "Hurry," she called. "I'd hate you to catch a cold because of me."

"Coming," said Grace. But she turned back to Waverley one last time. "I can't thank you enough. Without you, I would have drowned."

"I couldn't let that happen," said the mermaid. But, even in the moonlight, Grace could see that she looked worried. She was chewing her lip – exactly the way Scarlet would if she was about to go on stage or do a ballet exam.

"Is something the matter?" asked Grace. It didn't make any sense. Waverley had just saved her life. The young mermaid ought to look pleased and proud. Instead, she was squirming in the water, her glistening silver tail flicking anxiously from side to side.

"A mermaid is not allowed to save a drowning person from the waves," she said reluctantly. "I have broken the mermaid code."

"But that's silly!" Grace threw her arms in the air. "Surely you can't get into trouble for saving someone's life?"

"The sea must be repaid," said Waverley simply.

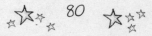

"Repaid? How?" asked Grace. "You don't have to throw me back in the water, do you?" She hoped making a silly joke might cheer the mermaid up.

But Waverley hung her head. "A gift of great value must be given to the sea," she said. "Or I will be banished from the water for ever."

"You mean you'll be forced to live on the land?" said Grace. The smile faded on her lips. "That's terrible." The beautiful, silver-tailed mermaid seemed as much part of the sea as a fish or a dolphin. "Do you have a gift of great value that you can give to the sea?" asked Grace "Will the other mermaids help you find one?"

"No. You don't understand." Waverley lifted her head and looked straight at Grace. "Because it was you that I rescued, it is you who must give the gift to the sea," she said.

"Me?" Grace was stunned.

"The gift must be something you own which was given to you freely and with love," said Waverley.

Grace's head was spinning. "I don't have anything valuable," she said. Although her father was a king, he was not as rich as most of the other royal families who sent their daughters to Tall Towers. Cragland was only a small, poor kingdom and Papa was a fair and honest ruler who spent his money on his people. Not like Precious's father, who charged high taxes to live grandly with his family while his people suffered.

Why couldn't it have been Precious who fell into the sea? thought Grace. She was so spoilt, her father had given her three different golden tiaras to choose from for just one party. If Waverley had rescued *her*, she would have endless jewels to toss into

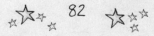

the sea. Super-wealthy Visalotta might be even better – she had boxes of diamonds and rubies in the way that other princesses had hair clips and buttons. Grace had nothing.

"The moon will be full in two nights' time," said Waverley. "You must bring your gift to Mermaid Rock then or I will be banished to the land for ever."

"In two nights' time?" said Grace, looking up at the night sky. How would she find a gift by then? The bright moon was almost a perfect circle already. Her heart was pounding like waves against a rock – but she didn't want to make Waverley any more worried than she already was. "I'll find something," said Grace firmly, leaping to her feet. "You saved my life. I'll make sure that you're not punished because of me."

"Hurry up, Grace, or you'll get a chill," called Scarlet. She had no idea what had been said, of course, and was waiting halfway across the beach, shifting anxiously from foot to foot.

"Coming," called Grace, hitching up her soggy nightie ready to run. She really ought to get back to the dormitory before Flintheart was up and about.

"One last thing," said the mermaid...

But her words were lost in the wind. Grace was already charging flat out across the sand. "Don't worry, Waverley," she called. "I won't let you down. I promise."

CHAPTER NINE
A Gift?

As they dashed across the gardens, Grace told Scarlet what Waverley had said about breaking the mermaid code and how she would be banished from the water for ever unless Grace could repay the sea with a valuable gift.

"But what will you do?" asked Scarlet, shocked.

"I don't know," said Grace as they crept back up the stairs to the dormitory.

"Perhaps everything will seem clearer in the morning," said Scarlet, kindly.

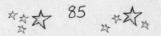

But Grace couldn't sleep a wink. She tossed and turned in her little white bed trying to think of anything valuable she could give to the sea. It would be terrible if, all because of her, poor Waverley lost her mermaid tail and was forced to live on the land like a human.

It would be like telling a bird that it couldn't fly, thought Grace. *Or a unicorn never being able to gallop.*

Exhausted, she finally dozed off and slept right through breakfast.

Scarlet was the same.

They might have slept all morning if Izumi, who had got up early to paint, hadn't dashed back up to the dormitory to shake them both awake.

The moment Grace's eyes were open, she yanked the drawer from her bedside table and tipped it out on the bed.

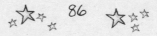

"I must have something valuable enough to give the sea," she said, as Scarlet explained to Izumi what had happened last night.

But it was hopeless. Grace scratched her head and sighed. There was the wrapper from a chocolate bar, a lock of Billy's hair, three bent safety pins, a ball of fluff and something that looked like it might once have been an apple core.

"Nothing!" she groaned. "The only really valuable thing I have is Billy. And I don't think he'd like to spend the rest of his life

living in the ocean like a seahorse!"

"I'll see if I have anything," said Izumi, stepping towards her dressing table.

"Thanks. But I don't think that'll work," said Grace. "Waverley said it had to be something of mine."

"It will be yours if I give it to you," said Izumi.

"As long as you don't actually ask anyone to give you something, I think it will be all right," said Scarlet as Izumi opened her jewellery box.

"Wow!" Grace gasped. There were strings of beads in every colour of the rainbow: ruby red, orange topaz, yellow amber, emerald green, sapphire blue, rose quartz and purple amethyst.

"They're so pretty," said Scarlet.

"But not valuable," sighed Izumi, shaking her head. "They're just things I made myself. The beads are only coloured glass. I love the

way they shine, but there's not a real jewel amongst them."

"I don't have any jewels either. No rubies or diamonds," said Scarlet, clutching the locket she always wore around her neck. "But this is real silver — it might be worth something. Take it if you think it will help." She undid the clasp and held the locket out.

"I couldn't," said Grace. "The first time I ever saw you take it off is when we went swimming."

"Use it if it will save Waverley," said Scarlet, still holding her hand towards Grace. "It's my fault you fell in the sea. If you hadn't followed me, you would never even have been on the beach."

"You're not to blame, honestly!" Grace raised her eyebrows. "You know what I'm like," she said. "I can trip over my own big feet without any help from anybody."

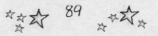

"I just can't bear the thought of Waverley being banished from the sea," said Scarlet. "It would be like someone telling me that I could never dance again." She didn't seem to notice that she was standing on pointed toes as she spoke.

"She looks so beautiful when she's in the water," nodded Grace, remembering how strong and wild the mermaid had seemed in the sea. "But are you sure you really want to give me this?" Grace touched the locket. It still felt warm from Scarlet's neck.

"If you think it will be enough," said Scarlet. "It belonged to my great-grandmother. But it's broken, I'm afraid. Nobody has been able to open it for years."

"If it's broken, then don't worry," Grace said gently. "The sea might not want it, and we don't want to take any chances." She wasn't sure this was true, but she couldn't

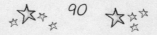

bear to risk Scarlet's beloved locket for nothing.

"I wish I was at home," said Izumi, as Scarlet clipped the locket back around her neck. "I have a few valuable things there, but my parents won't let me bring them to school."

"Like the birthday bracelet Visalotta gave you?" said Scarlet. "With real emeralds in your favourite shade of green."

Grace remembered the look of surprise on Izumi's face when she had unwrapped the gorgeous bangle at her birthday party last term. Visalotta was always generous. Even though she shared a dormitory with Precious, she never acted mean or spoilt in the same way.

"That bracelet really did look as if it was worth more than the whole of Cragland," said Grace.

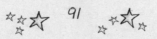

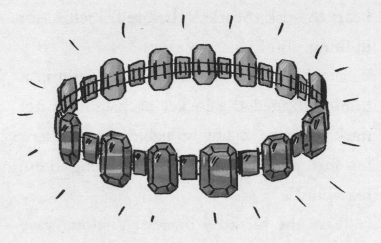

"Yet Visalotta's so rich she probably bought it with her pocket money," grinned Izumi, suddenly looking excited. "And it's your birthday tomorrow, Grace."

"Oh my goodness, that's true!" gasped Scarlet, smiling too.

"What?" said Grace, as her friends clapped their hands and spun her round the room.

"Don't you see?" asked Izumi.

"See what?" Grace frowned, stumbling to a dizzy stop.

"I know it feels horrible and greedy to even think like this," said Izumi. "But Visalotta is so generous, she's sure to give you something really valuable for your birthday too."

"You haven't asked her for anything, so the gift will be freely given, just like Waverley said it must be," added Scarlet.

"Do you really think she'll get me something?" Grace blushed. Izumi was right. It did feel horrible to expect a fancy present from another princess. But her heart was beating with excitement at the same time. Perhaps Visalotta's gift really would be something grand enough to offer to the sea. "I'd feel terrible if she did give me something valuable and I gave it away again," said Grace. "But it would be a real chance to save Waverley."

"We can explain once everything is all

right," said Scarlet. "Visalotta's so kind. I'm sure she will understand."

"Understand what?" said a voice outside the door.

The three friends jumped as Visalotta herself poked her head into the dormitory.

"Nothing," mumbled Grace, wishing she could be honest and beg Visalotta for help. But Waverley had warned that the gift must be something freely given, so Grace could not ask for anything.

"We were just talking about Grace's birthday party," said Izumi quickly. "She's having chocolate cake, of course."

"I certainly am," whooped Grace, licking her lips. The cooks at Tall Towers made wonderful cakes. She had asked for a chocolate sponge with chocolate cream inside and chocolate icing on top.

"And I hope you like surprises," grinned

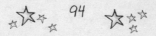

Visalotta. "Because I've got a big one for you!"

"A big surprise?" Grace felt her tummy flip.

"You'll have to wait till tomorrow to see what it is." Visalotta winked, disappearing through the door as the three friends gaped at one another.

"If Visalotta has promised you a big surprise, it will be something magnificent," whispered Izumi.

Grace chewed her fingernails. If she opened her presents at her birthday tea tomorrow, there'd still be enough time to deliver the gift to Mermaid Rock that night and save Waverley while the full moon was in the sky.

"Sorry!" Visalotta popped her head around the door again. "I nearly forgot why I came up here. Our swimming lesson has been

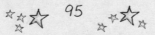

cancelled, so we're all supposed to go to the library. The mermaids aren't coming to school today."

"Waverley must be worried sick," sighed Grace, as Visalotta hurried away. "No wonder she's not coming to teach us – if I don't save her, this might be her last day in the sea."

CHAPTER TEN
The Library

The three friends found a quiet table in the far corner of the library.

Grace reached up for a sparkly, gold-covered book called *A Princess Guide to Jewels.*

"At least if there's no swimming, I can use the time usefully," she said. She really didn't know anything about which gems were valuable and which were not. If she was going to save Waverley, she was going to need something very precious indeed.

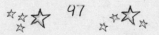

Crash! The book tumbled to the floor.

"Ouch!" yelped Grace as the heavy volume landed on her toe.

"Quiet!" scolded Fairy Godmother Flint. "You may read silently to yourselves. I have Sixth Formers to prepare for their Deportment Examinations and if I hear any bad reports from Fairy Godmother Webster there will be trouble." She scowled particularly hard at Grace.

"Quite so! Quite so!" The old librarian blinked sleepily as she lifted her head from her desk.

Flintheart wagged her finger at the First Years. "Not a peep!"

Grace breathed a sigh of relief as the teacher swept out of the room like an angry black buzzard. At least the mermaids hadn't told her what had happened last night. Grace couldn't bear to think what

98

sort of trouble she would be in. Now there was the hope, at least, that with Visalotta's gift she could put everything right.

Grace and Izumi each took a corner of *A Princess Guide to Jewels* and heaved open the cover.

"Diamonds are the most valuable stones of all," they read. Then they flicked over the page to look at pictures of rare pearls that had been harvested from the sea. It was strange to think that, by this time tomorrow, Grace might own something precious enough to appear in the pages of this book.

Not that I am going to keep the jewels for myself, she thought. That calmed her a little as she read how diamonds are mined from rocks deep in the ground.

Scarlet, meanwhile, was staring out of the window at the sea.

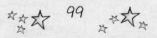

"What are you thinking about?" asked Grace.

Scarlet blinked as if she had been woken from a dream. "Can you two keep a secret?" she asked.

"Of course," said Grace. Izumi nodded and looked up from the book.

The other First Years were whispering in their own little groups of friends around the room. As long as nobody made too much noise, sleepy old Fairy Godmother Webster wouldn't wake up until the bell rang for the end of the lesson.

"Shhh!" Grace warned, putting her finger to her lips. Precious and the twins were on the table just the other side of the bookshelf. Peering through the gap where she had taken down the *Guide to Jewels*, Grace saw that Precious had grabbed the latest copy of *Throne Magazine* from the newspaper rack. She was pointing at pictures of a fancy

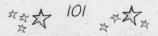

summer ball and sneering at the outfits the royal guests were wearing.

"Just look at the Queen of Geldland," Precious snorted. "Yellow really isn't her colour. She looks like she's fallen in a pot of custard."

The twins rocked with laughter.

"Perfect!" Grace knew that being horrid about other people's outfits would keep them happy for hours. It was safe to talk. "Go on," she said, smiling at Scarlet.

"Everything feels so strange at the moment," Scarlet began. "It's silly, but that day when I dived for the pearls, I..." She hesitated. "It was so odd. I've never learnt to swim but as soon as I was in the water I knew what to do. I almost felt like..."

"Like what?" said Grace, encouragingly.

"Like a mermaid!" Scarlet whispered, blushing pink as a pomegranate. "I felt like

I could have stayed in the water for ever. My legs were tingling — almost as if I was growing scales. That's why I'm so afraid. I feel as if the sea wants to trap me somehow."

"Like last night on the beach?" asked Grace. "You said it felt like the sea was calling to you."

"Yes." Scarlet looked close to tears. "It's stupid, but I keep checking my toes to see if I'm growing webbed feet or a scaly tail."

"Yuck!" There was a scream of laughter from behind Grace's head.

Grace turned to see Precious peering through the bookcase. How long had she been listening?

"Hey, everybody, Scarlet's turning into a fish!" Precious squealed.

"Shhhh!" said all the First Years at once.

"Be quiet," hissed Visalotta.

"You'll wake Fairy Godmother Webster," warned Princess Martine.

103

"Scarlet is *not* turning into a fish!" said Grace firmly.

"If anything, she's more like a mermaid," said Latisha excitedly. "She swims like one and she has such beautiful hair. . ."

"Ooh, yes," agreed Princess Rosamond. "Scarlet would make a gorgeous mermaid."

The princesses thought they were being kind, but poor Scarlet was squirming in her chair.

"Being a mermaid would be worse than being a fish," growled Precious. She was always jealous whenever Scarlet's beautiful red hair was praised. She picked up the copy of *Throne Magazine* and waved it in the air. "I don't see anyone in here with a tail, do you? It's not as if you could dance with a flipper. . ."

"Oh, for goodness' sake," said Grace.

But the twins squealed with laughter.

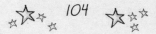

Fairy Godmother Webster sat bolt upright and blinked like an owl. "What's going on?" she asked, looking dazed.

"Nothing," mumbled the First Years, hurrying back to their seats. Everyone opened their books.

Before long, the Fairy Godmother dozed off again and Precious was happily poking fun at pictures of the Queen of Florabund's summer fête.

"That hat makes her look like she's got a flowerpot on her head," Precious jeered.

"I don't think for one minute you really are turning into a mermaid," whispered Grace, squeezing Scarlet's hand. "It's just like Waverley said — some people are drawn to the sea."

"I know," said Scarlet bravely. "And I feel so selfish thinking about myself when poor Waverley might be banished from her home for ever."

"But that won't happen," whispered Izumi. "Not now Visalotta has promised Grace a wonderful gift. That will be enough to save Waverley, I'm sure."

"I hope you're right," said Grace. She stood up and looked out of the window towards the beach. The Sapphire Sea was sparkling in the morning sunlight like the brightest gem in *A Princess Guide to Jewels*. All Grace could do now was wait until tomorrow to see what birthday gift Visalotta would bring.

CHAPTER ELEVEN
Back to Shell Beach

It was Saturday afternoon. Grace's birthday at last. Scarlet and Izumi had kept whispering to each other all morning.

"We have something we need to do," they told Grace, and they disappeared straight after lunch.

Grace had no idea where they had gone.

Now she was pacing up and down the dormitory, bubbling with excitement about her gifts and the birthday tea. But she felt sick with worry about Waverley too.

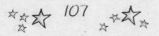

Her brain was whirling so fast, she felt as if it might explode like a party popper.

"There's only one thing for it," Grace said to herself out loud. She stamped her feet into her long riding boots, grabbed her hard hat and clattered down the stairs. A good gallop on Billy was the best way to clear her mind.

Billy thundered along the edge of the surf, salty spray splashing up into Grace's face as he galloped.

Suddenly, the little unicorn skidded to a stop and reared up on his hind legs.

Grace had to cling on to his mane. "What's the matter, boy?" she asked.

She was used to Billy skittering with excitement and playing about. But this was different. She could feel the brave, shaggy unicorn shaking with fear beneath her. His

 108

ears were pricked, listening. Grace stood up in her stirrups, straining to hear something too.

At first there was only the slap of waves and the rustle of wind in the long grass on the dunes. But then Grace heard a high wail, carried on the wind.

"Oooooohhh!"

"It's only a seagull, silly," said Grace, patting Billy's neck as a flock of birds swooped above their heads.

She squeezed her legs hard against his sides.

"Trot on!" she said.

But Billy wouldn't budge.

"Ooooohhh!" The high sad sound came again.

This time, Grace knew it wasn't a gull. "Waverley!" She saw the teenage mermaid lying close to the rocks where the princesses had played the shell game. "Are you all

right?" she asked, sliding down from Billy's back and leading him forward by the reins.

Waverley barely lifted her head. "Your friends were here just now," she said. "Over by the rock pool. But they didn't see me." Her blue eyes were pale and dim.

"Scarlet and Izumi? What were they doing on the beach?" said Grace.

"I'm not sure." Waverley shrugged. "It's funny, isn't it?" she said. "In stories, mermaids always long to come and live on the land."

"Yes," agreed Grace, realizing this was true. Ever since Mama had died, she always read bedtime stories to her little sister. One of Pip's favourites was about a mermaid who fell in love with a sailor and wanted to join him on the shore. There was another fairy tale about a mermaid and a prince.

"It's not like that in real life," said Waverley.

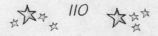

"At least not for me. I love the sea. I love swimming in the waves. I love my family and my underwater home."

"It must be wonderful," said Grace, her tummy twisting with guilt. Because of her, Waverley might be forced to leave all that behind.

Waverley lifted her head and there was light in her eyes again for a moment. "Next year, when I'm old enough, I'm going to enter the Seven Oceans Endurance Race," she said. "All the merfolk who take part must swim without stopping, from the time of one full moon until the next. Whoever swims furthest is the champion."

"I'm sure you could win," said Grace, remembering how fast Waverley had been when she was racing Latisha in the pool and how strong she had been the night she rescued Grace from the waves.

"That's why I was swimming so late when I saved you. I was training," said Waverley, pushing her hair out of her eyes. "Up until now, it has always been a merman who has won. I want to be the first mermaid."

"You could do it! I know you could," cried Grace, carried away with excitement.

But Waverley shook her head. "Not if I am living on the land. I won't be able to breathe like a mermaid any more."

"Oh..." Grace shuffled awkwardly, feeling silly not to have thought of that. As she looked down, she caught sight of Waverley's tail. It was dull and grey, almost camouflaged amongst the seaweed at the edge of the rocks. It was as if the mermaid was slowly dying at the thought of leaving the sea. All the brightness was going out of her. Her once-beautiful silver tail no longer shone and sparkled like diamonds in

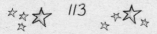

the sunlight. The scales were flaking away and it was as dry and cracked as an old leather boot.

Waverley flipped herself off the edge of the rocks and sank her shabby tail into the water as if she didn't want Grace to look at it. "I come from a long line of mermaids who have struggled to stay in the sea," she said. "A hundred years ago, there was a mermaid in my family who really did fall in love with a handsome young king. Just like something from a fairy tale. She had his baby, but she wouldn't join him on the land. She couldn't bear to leave the water, no matter how much she loved him. She raised their little daughter by herself. With the merpeople in the sea."

"What about the child?" asked Grace. "Did she grow up as a mermaid too? Did she stay in the sea for ever?"

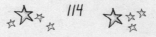

"Sadly, the mother died while she was still quite young," said Waverley. "We do not speak of what became of the child. It was all a long time ago."

"Gosh," said Grace. The story seemed so strange and secret, she longed to ask more questions.

But Waverley slipped deeper into the water, so that only her head and shoulders were above the waves. "I must go now," she said. "The other mermaids will worry where I am."

"Tell them everything's going to be all right," called Grace. "You won't have to lose your tail. You'll be strong enough to win the Seven Oceans Race. You see, it's my birthday. . ." She was desperate to explain that Visalotta had promised her a magnificent gift – but Waverley raised her hand.

"Just be here to meet me when the full moon is in the sky tonight," she said.

"I will," Grace promised. She saw a last flick of the mermaid's faded tail as she vanished leaving nothing but a stream of bubbles, which were carried away on the waves.

CHAPTER TWELVE
Getting Ready

Scarlet and Izumi refused to tell Grace what they had been up to on the beach. They were already dressed in their best party frocks by the time she got back to the dormitory, and they set about her with brushes, ribbons and combs.

"You'd better hurry and get dressed or you'll be late for your own birthday tea," said Izumi.

In spite of all her worries, Grace felt a buzz of excitement.

"Fairy Godmother Pom has made you a special frock," said Scarlet. The two friends pulled a crisp, new, navy-blue dress over the top of Grace's head.

"It's a sailor suit," said Grace, grinning as she caught sight of herself in the mirror. The kind school seamstress had always been fond of Grace. She knew her long, tall measurements off by heart, and the smart party dress with its wide collar and four white buttons was a perfect fit.

"I don't think I've ever liked a dress as much as this before," Grace beamed. She felt as if she could sail off across the high seas.

"Now all you need is shoes," said Izumi.

Grace glanced longingly at her comfy old riding boots, lying in a heap under the bed where she had just kicked them off. She knew her friends would shriek if she even so much as suggested those. "How about my slippers?" she teased.

"Luckily, they were washed away in the sea," laughed Scarlet.

"Then I'll have to wear my ballet pumps," smiled Grace. "They're the smartest thing I own."

She squeezed her long feet into the narrow satin shoes.

"Ouch!" she squealed. "I've grown again. These are squishing my toes."

"You do look really pretty though," smiled Scarlet.

"Like a proper princess?" asked Grace.

"Like a Tall Towers birthday princess,"

chorused Scarlet and Izumi together.

Grace took a last peek in the mirror and did a lopsided curtsy, which made her friends roar with laughter.

"Hurry, or we'll be late," said Izumi as the great clock on the tower struck five.

As they dashed down the stairs, they almost collided with Visalotta coming out of her dormitory.

"Don't look, I've got your present with me!" she said, hiding something behind her back.

Grace couldn't help noticing that whatever it was seemed very large.

"Shall I give you a clue?" grinned Visalotta, her eyes sparkling with cheeky joy. She was obviously delighted to be giving the perfect gift.

"Yes, please," said Grace, more desperate than ever to know what it might be.

"Let's see now," grinned Visalotta. "It melts

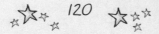

when it's made and makes drops of delight!"
She dashed away down the twisting staircase.
"That's the only clue I am going to give
you," she called.

"Melts when it's made?" whispered Grace.
"What do you suppose that means?"

"It might be something gold," said Izumi.
"They have to melt gold before they can
make it into jewellery."

"*Drops of delight* certainly sounds like gold
jewellery to me," said Scarlet. "Earrings,
perhaps."

"Golly," gulped Grace — but she felt her
heart soar. Fine gold would definitely be
enough to please the sea.

At last she could truly relax and enjoy
her party.

CHAPTER THIRTEEN
The Birthday Party

It was a Tall Towers tradition for the birthday princess to walk between two rows of classmates as they made an archway for her with their hands.

"Don't forget," Flintheart had reminded Grace that morning, "you must use the special procession walk you learnt in my deportment class. Bend your knees and count to three between each step."

"Yes," Grace promised. But the moment she spotted Fairy Godmother Pom, she

forgot all about it. She flung herself forward and flapped across the ballroom like a seagull in the wind. "Thank you for my sailor dress. I love it," she cried, spinning in a wobbly circle around the jolly seamstress.

"My pleasure, pet." Fairy Godmother Pom glowed with pride. "It fits you a treat, if I do say so myself."

"Congratulations on your birthday, Princess Grace," said Lady DuLac.

"Gosh, thank you." Grace spun round in quite the wrong direction and curtsied to a pillar by mistake.

"Best wishes, Young Majesty," added Flintheart sharply, without so much as a smile.

A great cheer rose up as the entire class burst into a chorus of "Happy Birthday" at the tops of their voices. Even Precious was mouthing the words and at least pretending to join in.

Grace looked up to the rafters and saw that they were hung with garlands of wild flowers. Over by the window, a long white table was laid with delicious-looking party food and big jugs of fresh, golden peach juice.

"Lead the way," smiled Lady DuLac, seeing Grace eyeing the treats. "After we have eaten tea, we can have party games and dancing."

"Then presents," winked Visalotta.

"I can't wait!" smiled Grace. She caught Scarlet's eye and they glanced down the long ballroom to where a small silver table was piled high with colourful gifts and packages. "Are those all for me?" gasped Grace in surprise.

"Of course they are, you daft duckling," said Fairy Godmother Pom, handing Grace a golden plate and steering her towards a giant wobbly jelly shaped like a unicorn. "Tuck in."

Grace had never seen party food that looked so wonderful — or tasted so scrumptious — ever before. Everything was unicorn-themed. Even the cucumber sandwiches were cut into a saddle shape. There were pink-icing horseshoe biscuits and pastry unicorn horns filled with wild strawberries, silver sprinkles and swirls of fresh cream.

"Yum!" Grace shivered with delight as she swallowed a spoonful of chilled pink pomegranate ice cream. "There are little marshmallow unicorns hidden in here," she beamed.

Just when she thought she couldn't eat another mouthful, the class burst into "Happy Birthday" again and four school cooks came down the stairs carrying an enormous chocolate birthday cake shimmering with candles.

"It is shaped like a unicorn too," grinned Grace.

"Not just any unicorn," said Izumi. "Look!" Grace saw that the cake had been decorated to look like Billy, with white and dark swirly chocolate icing to represent his white and black piebald patches. "It's brilliant!" she said.

"Don't forget to make a wish when you blow out the candles," said Lady DuLac.

Grace had already closed her eyes. Her fingers were crossed tightly behind her back for good luck. "Puuuuuuf!" She blew like the wind. "Please let me be able to save Waverley," she whispered under her breath. She opened her eyes as every candle flickered and went out.

That has to be a good sign, Grace thought. Her spirits soared as Scarlet and Izumi led her to the dance floor.

While the cake was being cut, they played musical chairs and danced so much that Grace's feet, squashed inside her narrow ballet shoes, felt as if they might fall off.

"And now for the presents," said Lady DuLac, when the girls had eaten slices of the rich, delicious, chocolatey cake.

Grace stepped forward. *This is it*, she thought. She was wobbling worse than a bowl of jelly.

Grace decided she would open Visalotta's gift first. She couldn't bear the suspense a moment longer.

But Precious pushed forward. "Open mine," she said, snatching a small package from the back of the stack. She seemed very excited and, for a moment, Grace wondered if the gift was something special that her aunt and uncle had bought for her.

One look at the smile on Precious's face made her guess differently though. Her cousin only ever got that look when she was about to do something mean.

"Happy birthday," said Precious, holding out a small crumpled package wrapped in lined paper that looked like it had been torn from one of her schoolbooks. "This might make you a bit more princessy, if you really try."

"Thank you," said Grace, intrigued. She wouldn't be surprised if Precious had wrapped up a frog or a toad. But, as she peeled back the crinkled paper, she saw a grubby wooden comb. It was old and used and chipped at one end. Precious had probably found it on the floor or under a bed somewhere.

"I thought it might be nice if you actually brushed your hair before school," sneered Precious, roaring with laughter.

The twins squealed with delight.

The gift was meant as a cruel joke – but Grace was delighted. "This is just what I need," she grinned, holding up the comb for everyone to see. The thick wooden teeth looked really strong. "I've been searching everywhere for just the right thing to get the knots out of Billy's mane. This is perfect, Precious. Thank you."

"You're welcome," scowled Precious, furious that her insult hadn't worked.

The twins giggled even harder as Grace opened a pack of boring, plain brown hair grips from them. They were obviously supposed to go with the comb.

"These will be really useful too," said Grace truthfully. She was forever losing hair clips and always ran out by the end of term no matter how many she had.

"Open ours next. It's something a bit

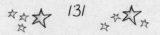

more fun," said Latisha, as she and Princess Martine tossed a huge round package through the air.

"Fantastic!" cried Grace. It was a giant beach ball. "I can't wait to play with this in the pool."

Princess Emmeline and Princess Christabel had got her a bright-red hay net to hang in Billy's stable. Princess Rosamond gave her a book of unicorn stories. And Princess Juliette had chosen a big bottle of pomegranate bubble bath with a unicorn-shaped sponge as well.

"Thank you for such perfect presents," said Grace.

"I'm surprised you don't turn into a unicorn," said Precious sulkily, looking down at the pile of thoughtful gifts as everyone crowded around.

"Mine doesn't have anything to do with

unicorns at all," Visalotta announced. "Why don't you open it next, Grace? I know you'll want to save Scarlet and Izumi's till last as they're your best friends." She smiled kindly.

"Ours is nothing, really," said Scarlet, pointing to a tiny blue box nestled among the few presents that were left. Grace saw that she was biting her lip. She wondered if Scarlet was nervous about her own gift or terrified that the present from Visalotta would not be enough to save Waverley after all.

"Good things often come in small packages," said Latisha.

"Not always," gulped Izumi. Visalotta had lifted up a huge red-velvet box as wide as a tea tray.

"Happy birthday, Grace," she grinned. "I hope this is what you want."

CHAPTER FOURTEEN
Visalotta's Gift

Grace's fingers were fluttering like fireflies as she took hold of the enormous velvet case. It had two gold clasps on the front. They were just the sort of thing that Grace had seen on jewellery boxes. But if this box really did contain something made of gold, it was big enough for a necklace, bracelets, earrings ... and a matching tiara too.

"I hope you haven't given Grace anything valuable," said Precious. "She looks like she's

about to tip the whole thing on the floor."

"Here. Let me help." Visalotta sprang forward. *Ping!* She flicked the gold clasps open as Grace held the crimson box. "Ready?" she asked.

"I think so," said Grace, but her voice sounded strange and squeaky like a mouse.

"Ta-da!" Visalotta lifted the lid with both hands.

"Wow!" Grace blinked as she stared down at the treasure chest that was revealed.

The inside of the box was velvet too, and row upon row of sparkling gems twinkled beneath the candlelit chandeliers. There was not just gold: shining silver, turquoise, green emerald and red ruby sparkled beneath her.

The colours were so bright it took Grace a moment to realize what she was looking at. "Chocolates," she said. "It's a box of chocolates!"

"Of course," beamed Visalotta, unwrapping the silver foil from a diamond-shaped truffle and popping it into Grace's mouth. "I was going to get you jewellery, but I know you

don't wear it – and you do love chocolate, don't you? I remember you telling Precious you'd rather have a box of chocs than any jewel in the world."

Grace had to smile. Visalotta had gone to such trouble to choose the perfect gift. How could she ever have guessed that, for once in her life, Grace wanted jewels more than anything else?

"Fank yoo!" she mumbled through the explosion of sweet, sticky caramel in her mouth. Visalotta's clue was exactly right – the little melting chocolate really was a drop of delight.

"Try a gold one next," said Visalotta.

Grace was strangely relieved that she wouldn't be able to give Visalotta's present away after all. It had never felt quite right. But that didn't mean she couldn't share it with her friends.

"Help yourselves, everybody," she said, passing the tray to Izumi. "There'll still be plenty for me." There were three whole layers of chocolates. "Thank you, Visalotta. I couldn't have wished for anything yummier."

But, as she licked a drop of sticky caramel from her fingers, Grace's throat felt dry. Chocolates had no place in the sea and, despite Visalotta's generosity, they weren't valuable. How would she save Waverley now?

CHAPTER FIFTEEN
Slippers and a Surprise

There were only two presents left for Grace to open.

One was a big, saggy-baggy, brown-paper package, which she knew must have come from home. The other was the tiny blue box from Scarlet and Izumi.

Grace lifted the little gift and rattled it beside her ear.

"Careful!" cried Scarlet.

"It's fragile," warned Izumi.

"Sorry!" Grace popped open the lid.

Inside, wrapped in soft, sandy-yellow tissue paper, were the three shells that the girls had found on the beach the day they went for a ride.

"That's why we went down to the beach this afternoon," explained Izumi. "It took us ages to find the shells again. Scarlet's was at the bottom of the rock pool."

"It's a friendship necklace," said Scarlet as Grace lifted the shells from the box. All three were strung together on a pretty sea-blue ribbon.

"A homemade present?" sneered Precious. "Is that it? I thought you were supposed to be her best friends!"

"It's a wonderful gift!" Grace was delighted. She looked at each of the three shells again, remembering how they were all so different, yet represented her and her two best friends so perfectly. "I love it!" she said.

"I'm afraid they won't be valuable enough to give to the sea," whispered Scarlet as she tied the ribbon around Grace's neck.

"I wouldn't give them away anyway," smiled Grace, trying not to panic now that she had opened all but her very last present.

The only gift left was the big, lumpy, bumpy package with a tartan bow on top.

"This one's from Papa," said Grace, certain that it would be no help either. She didn't even need to squeeze the parcel to guess

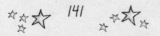

what was inside. "I know exactly what this will be," she said, ripping the paper to reveal a large fluffy pair of yak-hair slippers. "I get the same thing every year."

"You get slippers for your birthday every year?" laughed Precious. "Why don't you throw a tantrum?"

"I'd have a fit," squealed Trinket.

"Me too," squawked Truffle.

"Ooooh! They do look comfy," said Fairy Godmother Pom.

"They are," smiled Grace. "They're the comfiest slippers in the whole world. Back home in Cragland, you really do need something to keep your toes warm."

Grace sighed as a wave of sadness washed over her. Sometimes, she did secretly wish that she would get something different for her birthday. Poor Papa wasn't very good at knowing the sort of thing a princess

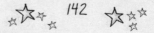

might want. Perhaps it would be different if Mama was still alive. But it wasn't the slippers that were making Grace sad; it was the thought of how much she missed Papa and her little sister, Pip. Birthdays at home were always so boisterous and noisy with Papa's warriors singing at the top of their voices. The party today was elegant and beautiful, but it could never be quite the same as being at home.

Grace caught sight of a rolled-up sheet of paper poking out of one of the slippers. She flattened it and saw that it was a handmade card from Pip. Her little sister had coloured in a picture of a unicorn and written "Happy Birthday" in the clouds. Grace felt more homesick than ever.

"What are you waiting for?" jeered Precious. "Aren't you going to put the slippers on?"

That did it. She wasn't going to let Precious make fun of her for a moment more. "I'm going to put them on right now, actually," she said. "My feet are killing me!" Grace kicked off her tight ballet shoes and plunged her foot inside the first slipper, feeling how soft and furry it was.

"One last dance and then it's time to go up to bed," said Lady DuLac, glancing outside at the darkening sky.

Grace froze. The moon would be up in less than an hour and she still had no gift valuable enough to give the sea.

Pulling on the second slipper, she stumbled to the window to look out at the sky. "Ouch!" Her toes bashed against something hard and sharp. "What's that?" she said, hopping on one foot as she held on to Scarlet's shoulder. She pulled the slipper off. There was a clatter as something fell to the floor.

Grace leant down and picked up a white leather pouch. It was surprisingly heavy.

"It must be an extra gift," said Lady DuLac. "I expect your father slipped it inside the slipper to keep it safe."

"But what could it be?" said Grace as she weighed the pouch in her hand. The white leather was as soft as velvet. There was a label and she flipped it over, expecting to see Papa's big messy handwriting scrawled across the card. Instead, she saw rows of small tidy letters in blue ink, so neat that even Flintheart would have given four merit points to any Tall Towers princess with handwriting like it.

Grace blinked, tears filling her eyes. "It's from Mama," she said. She was so surprised, she nearly dropped the pouch all over again.

"Steady," said Lady DuLac, holding Grace's arm.

"My mother must have written this for me before she died," said Grace. Seeing the handwriting jolted her memories of Mama as clearly as if she had smelt a waft of the lily-of-the-valley perfume she always used to wear. Grace read the label aloud. As she spoke, she could hear Mama's bright, bubbly voice in her mind:

Darling Grace,
This necklace belonged to your Great-Grandmother Joy. It was given to me when I was your age. I only wish I could be there to see you put it on. Giving is a far greater gift than receiving.

Always remember that.
Love, Mama. x

A tear rolled down Grace's cheek. Mama must have known she was dying when she wrote this note.

"What does she mean, Great-Grandmother Joy's necklace?" screeched Precious. "What necklace? If it is anything valuable, it ought to belong to me. Joy was my great-grandmother too. And I am the oldest cousin..."

Grace ignored Precious. She had never heard of Mama having anything valuable anyway.

Wouldn't it be wonderful if it was a little locket like the one Scarlet has, she thought. *With a picture of Mama inside.* But the pouch seemed too heavy for that. She tipped it upside down and held out her hand to catch whatever was inside.

There was a flash of silvery light.

"Oooh!" A cry of wonder went up from every princess in the room.

Even Lady DuLac let out a gasp of surprise.

Grace stared down at the shimmering, shiny necklace in her hand. The silvery stones shone so brightly, she felt as if she was holding a string of stardust in her fingers.

"Diamonds?" screamed Precious. "Your mother gave you diamonds?"

"Yes," gulped Grace, holding up the biggest, heaviest, shiniest necklace she had ever seen.

CHAPTER SIXTEEN
The Diamonds

The First Years crowded around Grace to admire the jewels.

"It's the most beautiful necklace ever," said Princess Martine.

"There must be two hundred diamonds on it," cried Princess Juliette.

Grace gulped. She was still in a state of shock.

"Aren't you going to try it on?" asked Visalotta.

"Yes. Take off that silly homemade necklace," said the twins.

"You're not going to want shells now you have diamonds," sighed Precious.

"That's not true," said Grace. "I love the shells." But Scarlet had already reached up to untie the ribbon.

Izumi lifted the diamonds and helped Grace with the clasp. "Look!" She spun Grace round so that she could see herself in the huge gold mirror on the ballroom wall. "You're just like an empress!"

"Golly!" Grace's jaw dropped open. She couldn't believe quite how big and shiny the diamonds really were – each one like a frozen teardrop. The necklace was so heavy it made Grace stoop her shoulders. As she looked at herself in the mirror, there was a little part of her that secretly wished that she was still wearing the simple shells. The diamonds made her feel as if her reflection belonged to someone else. Izumi was right.

 150

The jewels should be worn by an empress –
Grace had enough trouble trying to be a
proper princess, let alone someone even more
royal than that.

"This is SO unfair!" roared Precious,
stamping her feet. "I am two months older
than you. If these diamonds belonged to
Great-Grandmother Joy, then I ought to have
them, not you."

"But you've got the pearls," said Grace, pointing to the string of beautiful beads around Precious's neck. "They belonged to our great-grandmother too."

"Pearls!" Precious looked like she had swallowed a sour onion. "Why would I want boring pearls when I could have sparkling diamonds?" With a sudden movement she tore the pearl necklace from round her neck and hurled it across the floor.

"Gracious me!" cried Fairy Godmother Pom as the twins went scuttling after the bright white string of beads like fluffy kittens chasing a ball of wool.

"That is quite enough, Young Majesty," said Flintheart, wagging her finger at Precious. "You need to calm down."

"But it's not fair. Grace doesn't deserve anything as pretty as diamonds," wailed Precious, stamping her feet. "She'll lose them somewhere."

 152

"Princess Precious, this is not the proper way to behave," said Lady DuLac. "I am sure Grace realizes what a wonderful gift she has been given and will look after the diamonds with great care."

"Of course," choked Grace, but she felt a stab of guilt, so strong it made it hard to breathe. The diamonds really were the most valuable gift she had ever been given. Not just because they were worth so much money but because they were from her mother. Even if they had been wooden beads she would have treasured the necklace dearly. She wished she could have seen Mama wear them. She must have looked so beautiful. Grace touched the diamonds, hoping they might bring her memories of Mama to life in some way. But the bright stones felt cold.

Grace knew she could not keep the diamonds, no matter how much she wished

153

she could. She looked down at her cousin lying on the floor kicking her feet in a tantrum. What would Precious say if she discovered Grace was going to toss the diamonds into the sea?

"I have no choice," whispered Grace to herself. "I have to save Waverley tonight."

CHAPTER SEVENTEEN
Journey Across the Waves

The full moon shone high in the sky as Grace, Scarlet and Izumi stood side by side on the silvery sand. They stared out across the sea towards Mermaid Rock, its spiky trident shape casting three long shadows across the shimmering midnight water.

"Thank you for coming with me," said Grace, putting her arms around her friends as they watched the waves, waiting for Waverley to appear.

Scarlet let out a tiny whimper. "I just

wish I wasn't so nervous," she said, leaping backwards as a wave splashed on to the shore.

"You'll be fine," laughed Grace. "I think you're actually braver than the rest of us put together." It was true. Scarlet was always afraid of new things, but whenever real courage was needed she had nerves as strong as a suit of armour. Grace knew she would never have left her to come and rescue Waverley alone.

"That's right, Scarlet," chuckled Izumi. "Remember how you were the first one to jump on the dragon's back the time Grace saved us from the cliffs?"

"And it was you who stood up to Precious when she was bullying me in our first term," said Grace.

Scarlet shuffled with embarrassment. "I'm just glad we're all here together tonight," she said. "To keep each other safe."

"I wouldn't have missed it for the world," said Izumi. "I'm longing to see what Mermaid Rock is really like."

"It is going to be an adventure, isn't it," smiled Grace. "Now we have the diamonds we can enjoy ourselves. We know we can save Waverley for sure."

"I wish we had a different gift we could offer the sea," sighed Scarlet.

"It seems so sad you have to give your mother's necklace away," Izumi agreed.

"It's the right thing to do," said Grace bravely. But the necklace was the only thing of Mama's she'd ever been given. To hand the diamonds on so soon was going to break her heart. She ran her fingers over the precious stones around her neck. She hadn't taken them off since the birthday party and they felt warmer now, pressed against her skin. "At least they're clipped

 157

on tight," she smiled. "It would be just like me to lose them before we even get to Mermaid Rock."

"Don't even say that!" gasped Scarlet. She had taken off her own locket and left it safely in the dormitory before they came down to the beach. The girls had changed into their swimming costumes just in case they had to swim all the way out to the rock.

"I'm sure Waverley will bring a boat for us," said Grace, feeling Scarlet trembling beside her as they stared at the sea.

"Hello," called a high clear voice, and Grace saw the splash of a tail above the waves.

"That doesn't sound like Waverley," she said.

A moment later Oceana slid on to the shingle. "We must hurry," said the older teacher. "Waverley is too weak to swim. She's waiting at Mermaid Rock – we don't have a moment to lose."

 *158*

"How do we reach the rock?" asked Scarlet, no longer able to hide the terror in her voice. It was clear that Oceana had not brought a boat.

Even Grace felt nervous. She knew the mermaid teacher would look after them, but the rock was a very long way from the shore. "Look!" she cried. Three dolphins were leaping through the waves towards them.

"You must call them to you," said Oceana. "You're going to ride on their backs."

Grace felt a flash of excitement. She had ridden a unicorn many times, of course. And a dragon once. But never a dolphin. "Come on, dolphins," she cooed.

But the dolphins ignored her.

"They won't come to you like that," said Oceana, with an impatient flip of her tail. The anxious teacher was clearly desperate to head back to Waverley as quickly as they could. "You have to sing for them."

"Sing? Oh no!" Grace cleared her throat. "*Dolphins, coo-ee! Come here,*" she warbled. Her voice was carried back to her on the wind. It sounded as if a seagull was trying to be sick. "*Come, lovely dolphins, come here,*" she sang again. But, instead of swimming closer, the gentle creatures turned and fled back out to sea. "I don't think they liked that much," said Grace. But then Scarlet stepped shyly forward and began to sing.

Oh come, leaping dolphins, oh steeds of
the sea,
Oh come to the shore now, oh come
carry me.

Grace had never heard Scarlet's voice sound so beautiful. Instantly, the dolphins turned and began to swim back towards the shore.

"Well done, Scarlet! How did you know what to sing?" gasped Izumi.

"I—I'm not sure." Scarlet looked as surprised as anybody. "Isn't it a nursery rhyme or something? I think I heard it when I was a little girl."

"It is an old mermaid tune," said Oceana, who was circling a little way offshore. She stared at Scarlet with her head on one side. "It is rare for someone from the land to know the words."

"Look!" whispered Grace.

The three silvery-blue dolphins had swum to the shallow water.

"Climb on!" said Oceana. "We must hurry."

The dolphins made soft clicking sounds, as if to reassure the girls that everything would be all right. Poor Scarlet still looked terrified as she stepped into the edge of the sea and water lapped over her toes.

"You don't have to come if you don't want to," said Grace. "Honestly, I'll be fine."

Scarlet shook her head. "It is my fault Waverley broke the mermaid code to rescue you in the first place. I should be with you when you give the gift to the sea."

"Here goes then," said Grace. The three girls held hands and splashed through the shallow water towards the waiting dolphins.

The moment she was on the dolphin's back, Grace knew she was going to enjoy the ride.
Whoosh!
They were off.
Grace's dolphin leapt high out of the water.

"Yippee!" she cried, holding the dolphin's fin with one hand and clutching the diamonds around her neck with the other. It was just like riding Billy bareback except that the dolphin was slippery. Grace had to grip tight with her knees as they soared over the waves.

Grace's dolphin was the fastest of the three. Izumi's was just behind her, but Scarlet's went more slowly, hanging back beside Oceana, as if sensing that its rider was afraid.

Soon, the steep, wet walls of Mermaid Rock rose out of the water ahead of them, glistening like an enchanted palace in the moonlight.

The dolphins slowed and began to circle round and round in the water.

"Thank you," said Grace, patting her dolphin's smooth head. He turned and nuzzled her with his long grey nose.

Grace looked up at the bright full moon, all the excitement of the ride still bubbling inside her.

"I can't believe it," she smiled as Scarlet's dolphin bobbed alongside. "We're going to be able to save Waverley – and we get to visit Mermaid Rock too."

CHAPTER EIGHTEEN
Mermaid Rock

"We are here. You rode well, Young Majesties," said Oceana. She smiled encouragingly, but her tail was flicking from side to side beneath the water. Grace sensed she was more anxious than ever. "The Mermaid Queen is waiting inside," she said, pointing to an archway at the base of Mermaid Rock. "You will need to swim under water for a few moments. When you come up on the other side, you will find yourself in the Royal Grotto."

"Like a secret cave?" asked Grace, patting her dolphin one last time and sliding off his back.

"Exactly," said Oceana. "Hurry now!"

"Don't worry, Scarlet. I'll go first," said Grace, looking round, expecting her friend to be scared.

But Scarlet had already dived into the water and disappeared.

"Wait!" cried Izumi.

But Grace knew there was no time to lose. "Come on," she said.

They plunged downwards together, following the ripples that Scarlet had left behind.

Once they were through the archway, Grace swam upwards towards a circle of light. She gasped as she broke through the surface of the water. Just as Oceana had promised they were inside a grotto, but Grace hadn't

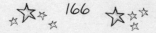

expected anything as large and beautiful as this. Scrambling out on to the polished mother-of-pearl floor, she saw that the walls and ceiling of the cave were covered in swirling mosaics of brightly coloured shells. The top of the high roof was open to the sky and directly below was a perfect round pool of clear blue water. In the stillness of its surface Grace could see the full moon reflected like a shining lantern.

Scarlet was standing at the edge of the pool. Grace and Izumi glanced at each other. They had never seen her so bold before. Scarlet normally hung back, shy to show herself in new places. But she stepped forward and curtsied to a golden-tailed mermaid in a shining crown. Grace guessed this must be the Mermaid Queen.

"Greetings, Your Majesty," Scarlet said.

Izumi bobbed down elegantly beside her

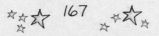

and Grace tried her best to do the same, but her wet feet kept slipping on the shiny floor. She toppled backwards and clutched hold of Izumi's arm. As she landed in a tangled heap, she wished she could have an elegant, shiny tail like a mermaid instead of her long, skinny legs with knobbly knees. They looked more gangly than ever poking out from her swimsuit.

Izumi helped her up and Grace tried her best to curtsy all over again. "I am sorry for the trouble I have caused, Your Majesty," she said.

"Shhh!" The royal mermaid raised her finger to her lips. "What is done is done. Now we must do all we can to help Waverley." She gestured to the side of the pool.

Waverley was lying motionless on the far side of the water. Her once-dazzling tail was as flaked and dry as ashes in a

burnt-out fire. She barely lifted her head as she whispered, "Hello, friends!" Her eyes flickered with hope for a moment as she smiled at Grace.

"Don't worry. Everything's going to be all right," Grace said. She felt her heart leap. Now she had the diamonds she could save Waverley for sure. The teenage mermaid would be back in the water training for the Seven Oceans Race before the next full moon.

"I am proud of what Waverley did," said the queen. "She was right to save you from the water. But the sea is a cruel mistress. I hope you have a gift great enough to repay your debt and free Waverley from the dreadful punishment of living on the land."

The merfolk who were gathered on the rocks around the pool let out a slow, sad moan.

"For us, there is no fate worse than to

leave the ocean for ever," said a dark-haired merman with a silver spear.

"Don't worry. I have the perfect gift," said Grace. Seeing Waverley so helpless, she was more certain than ever that this is what Mama would have wanted her to do with the diamonds.

Scarlet was still staring silently into the pool but Grace glanced at Izumi, who gave her a bright smile of encouragement.

"Come, stand here by the Returning Pool," said Oceana, leading Grace to the edge of the circle of clear water.

"Returning Pool?" said Grace. "What an odd name. Why is it called that?" But the mermaids were singing now and nobody seemed to hear her.

"You must read these words," said a merman handing Grace a scroll. "Then slip your treasure gently into the pool."

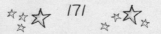

"*Gently*," Grace nodded. "Got it!"

The merfolk's singing rose higher and higher as everyone stared at her. Grace gulped. She hadn't realized there would be some sort of ceremony.

"Sorry!" Grace blushed as she fumbled to untie a ribbon of seaweed from around the scroll. She cleared her throat and read the words in her best loud voice, which seemed to echo all around the rocky grotto:

> *I give thanks, kind mermaid, for saving me*
> *And offer this gift to repay the sea*
> *Given freely with love, this treasure*
> *once mine*
> *Shall return to the sea till the end*
> *of time.*

Grace reached up to undo the clasp of her necklace, struggling to get it undone.

She tried not to think of how beautiful the diamonds were or what they might have meant to Mama. The only thing that mattered now was saving Waverley.

"Wait," cried the queen leaning forward as the bright reflection of the diamonds shimmered on the water. "Is that the gift you intend to give?"

"Yes," Grace nodded. "Is something wrong?" But at that moment, the clasp came undone and the necklace fell from her neck. There was a loud splash as the diamonds sank into the pool.

Waverley let out a low moan.

"Whoops!" Grace turned desperately towards the queen. The royal mermaid was shaking her head. "I'm sorry – that wasn't very gentle," said Grace. "My fingers slipped." As she spoke the water in the pool began to bubble and swirl.

CHAPTER NINETEEN
The Returning Pool

"What's happening?" cried Grace.

The water was churning so fast it was as if a giant whirlpool had sprung up beneath the floor of the grotto.

"Look out!" Grace grabbed Scarlet's arm and pulled her back from the edge of the pool just as a huge fountain of water spurted up like a tidal wave. "The diamonds!" Grace saw a flash as something bright and shiny flew above the spray.

The necklace was thrown high into the

air. There was a streak of silver light like lightning as the jewels were tossed out of the pool. Grace was still holding Scarlet's arm, but she let go and scrabbled on the floor, grabbing the diamonds as they shot past her.

Just as quickly as the whirlpool had begun, the waters settled and cleared.

"Did it work?" Grace spun around to look at Waverley.

The mermaid's eyes were closed and her face was still. Her poor, ragged tail was twitching – like a fish desperate to return to the water.

"I don't understand," gasped Grace. This was worse than she could have imagined. The sea seemed somehow angry with the gift of the diamonds – it had thrown them from the pool as if they were worthless glass.

And Waverley looked worse than ever.

"Let me try again," said Grace, turning towards the queen. "I'll be more careful this time. I'll slide them into the pool really gently, without so much as a splash."

"I am afraid there is no point." The queen flicked her mighty golden tail. "The sea does

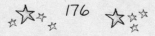

not want your gift," she said sadly.

"The sea doesn't want it?" Grace stared down at the shimmering diamonds in her hands. "But this necklace is the only valuable thing I own," she said. "I don't have anything else." She had never for a moment dreamed that the precious diamonds would not be enough to save Waverley.

"Although your diamonds are a valuable and generous gift," said the queen, "they are of the land."

"Of the land?" echoed Grace. "What do you mean?"

"Diamonds are dug from rocks under the ground," said the Mermaid Queen.

"That's right." Izumi came to stand next to Grace. "We read about that in the library. Do you remember? *A Princess Guide to Jewels* explained how diamonds are mined from deep in the earth."

Grace nodded. "But what does it matter if diamonds are of the land?" she said desperately. "This necklace was given to me freely and with love, just as Waverley said it should be." She held up the necklace. "These diamonds belonged to my mother and my grandmother and great-grandmother before that."

"The love from them is great. I can feel that," said the queen. "But your gift must be something that comes from the sea. Did Waverley not explain?"

"Oh dear," said Waverley weakly. "I called out to you, Grace. The night I saved you. But you were back on the beach. Perhaps you didn't hear me."

"Oh no!" Grace remembered Waverley had shouted something, but she had already been charging across the sand towards Tall Towers, desperate to be back in the dormitory before Flintheart caught them out of bed.

"For all their beauty, your diamonds could never have saved Waverley," said the queen. "If only I had known they were what you planned to give. The sea has no need of them. The gift must be something that was once taken away from the water and is now *returned* there to repay your debt."

"How can I have been so stupid?" Grace groaned, thinking of the words she had just read out from the scroll.

Given freely with love, this treasure once mine
Shall return *to the sea till the end of time.*

That was why the Returning Pool had such a strange name. The magical waters were intended to receive precious gifts back to the sea — to *return* them to where they had come from in the first place.

"But I don't have anything that came from the sea," said Grace.

"It is hopeless then," said the proud queen and she crumpled she as if she was about to cry. "I shall miss poor Waverley dreadfully when she is banished to the land."

Grace swallowed. She felt her own eyes fill up with tears. This was all her fault. If only she had listened more carefully.

"But, wait!" Waverley cried out. "I feel a little stronger." Her voice was clear and her eyes were bright.

"That's wonderful!" Grace clapped her hands. She could see the mermaid's tail was glowing softly now with speckles of silver amongst the dull grey scales once again. "Perhaps the diamonds did the trick after all!" she cheered. She turned back to the queen. "Do you think that can be true?"

But the queen shook her head. "It is not

the diamonds that have helped. Look." She pointed towards the Returning Pool.

Grace spun round. "Scarlet!" she cried.

The red-haired princess was standing in the middle of the water.

"Quickly, get out of the pool!" said Grace, her heart pounding.

But Scarlet was singing softly to herself with the same faraway expression on her face that Grace had seen the night she followed her to the beach.

"It is too late," said the Mermaid Queen. "Scarlet has offered herself to the sea as a gift."

"That's why I am growing strong again," said Waverley, tears streaming down her face. "The pool has taken Scarlet to pay your debt."

Grace felt as if she had been punched in the stomach.

"My legs feel strange," said Scarlet. Her voice was tired but she sounded quite calm.

"No!" cried Izumi.

Grace dashed forward and peered into the clear blue water of the pool. Below the surface, she could see the shape of Scarlet's long pale legs. Only they weren't pale white any more – they were glowing silver, as if someone had sprinkled them with diamonds. "Oh, Scarlet," gasped Grace, remembering her friend's worst fears. "You're turning into a mermaid."

CHAPTER TWENTY
A Prisoner in the Pool

"I can't move," gasped Scarlet. "I don't understand what is happening."

"It is clear you have mermaid blood in you," said the queen gently. "Some of your ancestors must have been merfolk. Now the sea wants you to return to the water."

"But I don't want to be a mermaid," said Scarlet, looking really frightened now. "My home is on the land. With my family ... and my friends." She looked at Grace and Izumi.

"How do we stop this?" cried Grace, wishing

she could just splash into the Returning Pool and carry Scarlet out. But the strange silvery light flickering on the surface told her that was hopeless. The sea had control of Scarlet now.

"By stepping into the pool, Scarlet acted freely and with love," said the queen.

"She returned to the water like her mermaid ancestors and freed me from being sent to the land," said Waverley, her tail shimmering. "I would have stopped her if I'd known what she was going to do."

"I don't think you could have stopped me," said Scarlet, with a small, sad smile. "The sea was calling to me so loudly it was the only voice I could hear."

"But you're not a mermaid yet," said Grace. She could still see the shape of her friend's long pale legs in the water. "Do something!" she pleaded with the queen. "Surely there's still time to stop the change from happening."

"I am afraid there is nothing I can do," said the queen. "Just as I could not save Waverley, I cannot help Scarlet either. It is you who has the power, Grace."

"Me?" Grace blinked.

"In changing places with Waverley, Scarlet has paid your debt to the sea," said the queen. "It is you who was saved from the water in the first place."

"Of course." Grace felt tears prick her eyes. This terrible mess was all her fault.

"You must think clearly and act fast," said the queen.

"Anything! Just tell me what to do." Grace threw her shoulders back, instantly ready to help. "I'll even become a mermaid if I must." She stepped forward towards the pool.

The queen held up her hand. "You are very brave," she smiled kindly. "But, as far as I know, you do not have mermaid blood."

"No." Grace felt her shoulders crumple. "The sea would not want me. But what can I do? How can I save Scarlet?"

"With a gift, of course," said the queen. "There is still time. Find something of great value and offer that to take Scarlet's place."

"Oh, Grace," said Scarlet. "I want to go home. I want to go back to Tall Towers. . ."

"I'll find something," said Grace, but she felt as if she was trapped on a hopeless merry-go-round. First she had been asked to save Waverley, and now, Scarlet ... but the only gift she had was the diamonds. And the sea did not want them.

The queen clicked her fingers and beckoned to the merman with the spear. "Swim to shore," she ordered him. "Raise the alarm. Tell Lady DuLac everything that has happened here tonight. I know she will help her princesses in any way that she can."

"Yes, Your Majesty."
The merman dived under the
archway that led back out to sea.

"You must go too," said the queen, turning
briskly to Grace and Izumi. "Scarlet will be
safe with us. Trust yourself, Grace. Find a
gift that is of the sea, bring it back and set
Scarlet free."

"But how long do I have to find something?" said Grace, looking towards the pool. Scarlet seemed to have sunk lower in the water.

"The moon will be full for just one more night," said the queen, glancing up through the open roof to the sky above. "To save Scarlet, you must return here with your gift by midnight tomorrow."

CHAPTER TWENTY-ONE
Stories From the Past

It was dawn as Grace and Izumi rode their dolphins to the shores of Coronet Island. As they neared the beach, they could see Lady DuLac at the edge of the waves, talking to the merman with the spear.

"He will have explained everything," said Oceana, swimming beside them.

"Thank goodness you are safe, Young Majesties," cried the headmistress as they patted their dolphins and splashed through the water towards her. "Thank you for

bringing them home safely, Oceana." Lady DuLac spoke quickly to the mermaid teacher, then led Grace and Izumi all the way up to their little white bedroom at the top of the Dormitory Tower. "You have not slept all night. You must rest for a while," she insisted, "or you will be no help to Scarlet at all."

"But..." Grace tried to object. They had so little time – just a single day before darkness fell again for the last night of the full moon.

"I have sent for Scarlet's parents," said Lady DuLac. "They will be here in a few hours. When they arrive, we will decide exactly what to do."

"No arguments," said Flintheart, who was waiting in Sky Dorm, pacing up and down like an angry crow.

Fairy Godmother Pom appeared with cups

of steaming hot chocolate. She tucked the girls into bed as they explained everything that had happened.

"It is all my fault," said Grace. "I should have asked for your help the first time I saw Scarlet heading down to the beach."

"It was a very dangerous thing to do," said Flintheart. And Grace knew, for once, that her strict form teacher was right.

Lady DuLac sat on the little chair beside Grace's bed. Grace couldn't help wishing she had tidied away the dirty socks and the wrinkled old cardigan that were hanging from the back.

"I am glad you understand the dangers you have put yourself in," said Lady DuLac, "but I should have foreseen that something like this might happen."

"You?" said Grace. "How?"

"I was aware of Scarlet's family history,"

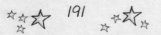

191

said Lady DuLac. "I knew that she had mermaid blood."

"You knew?" Grace was shocked. "I don't think even Scarlet knew before tonight."

"Or her parents," said Izumi. "Surely they would have told her if they did?"

"It was kept secret," said Lady DuLac, "to protect the family name."

"Why would they care?" asked Grace but, even as she spoke, she remembered how rude Precious had been about the merfolk.

"Attitudes have mostly changed now," said Lady DuLac. "But once upon a time there was a lot of prejudice."

"And you'd be surprised," sighed Fairy Godmother Pom. "There are still some foolish folk who think pure royal blood is more important than how well you rule your kingdom."

"We don't stand for any of that sort of nonsense in this school," said Flintheart. "It is how a princess behaves, not who her ancestors are, that matters."

Grace smiled. She had always been so afraid of Fairy Godmother Flint. For the first time, she realized the form teacher had a good heart.

"Sorry, Lady DuLac," said Izumi, blushing, "but I don't understand. I mean ... if Scarlet's history is such a secret, then ... well, how do you know about it?"

"As headmistress of Tall Towers, you would be surprised by the things I know," smiled Lady DuLac. "Royal families have been sending their daughters to this school for hundreds of years. There are whole rooms in Headmistress Tower piled high with files and boxes, some dating back to the very beginning of this academy.

There are letters, school magazines, class lists, enrolment scrolls – every piece of parchment in those rooms tells a story. Often, they are things that people do not speak of."

"The walls of Tall Towers could tell many tales," agreed Fairy Godmother Pom.

"And Scarlet's secret goes back generations," continued Lady DuLac. "Her parents may not know about the mermaid blood. Nor even her grandparents. But there is an old story from a hundred years ago..."

"I think I've heard it..." Grace sat up in bed so fast she spilled hot chocolate down the front of her nightdress. "Waverley told me... Was that Scarlet's relation? The one who was a mermaid?"

Lady DuLac nodded.

Grace gasped and grabbed Izumi's hand.

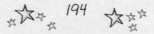

"Many years ago a mermaid fell in love with a handsome young king," she said. "She had his baby, but she wouldn't join him on the land. She couldn't bear to leave the water so she raised their little daughter by herself. With the merpeople in the sea."

"That means the baby must have been half human, half mermaid," said Fairy Godmother Pom.

"But what happened to her?" said Izumi.

"I don't know." Grace turned back towards the headmistress. "I asked Waverley, but she said the same thing as you, Lady DuLac. She said it is something the merfolk do not speak of."

"Her name was Turquoise," said Lady DuLac.

"Her mother died while she was still young," remembered Grace.

 195

"That's right." Lady DuLac laid her hand gently on Grace's shoulder. "I know you will understand how that feels," she said. "Turquoise did not want to stay in the sea once her mother was gone. She swam near the shore every day hoping to hear news of her father. One evening, she was close to Coronet Island when a young princess from Tall Towers was washed into the sea. She would have drowned if Turquoise had not saved her."

"Turquoise broke the mermaid code," gasped Grace. "If she rescued the princess she would be banished from the sea – just like when Waverley saved me."

"But remember, Turquoise felt a longing for the land," said Lady DuLac. "She wanted to find her father, the king."

"So she became human and left the sea for ever," said Grace. "By breaking the mermaid

196

code she set herself free from the water."

"Exactly," said Lady DuLac. "And she soon found her father. He was king of a small island in the Southern Ocean, which meant that she was *Princess* Turquoise, of course. By the start of the summer term, she was a pupil here at Tall Towers, just as she had wished. You can see her name on all the scrolls and class lists from that time."

"What a wonderful story!" sighed Fairy Godmother Pom. "I hope she became friends with the princess she rescued."

"The very best of friends," smiled Lady DuLac.

"And what was the name of the princess Turquoise saved?" asked Grace.

"Ah, I was wondering when you would ask me that," smiled Lady DuLac, reaching into the pocket of her robe. "Perhaps you ought to have a look at this." She handed

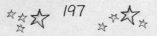

Grace a big gold coin pinned to a faded blue ribbon.

"It looks like an old medal," said Grace, turning the coin over in her hand.

"Read the inscription," prompted Lady DuLac.

The letters carved on the old medal were so curly it took Grace a moment or two to decipher what they said. But as she made the words out, her eyes grew wide:

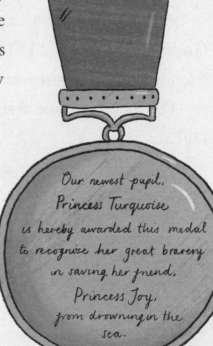

Our newest pupil, Princess Turquoise is hereby awarded this medal to recognize her great bravery in saving her friend, Princess Joy, from drowning in the sea.

"Joy? But that was my great-grandmother's name," said Grace. "Does that mean...?"

'Yes." Lady DuLac smiled.

"Gosh! So Scarlet's great-grandmother saved my great-grandmother's life." Grace grinned. "And they became best friends. Imagine that!"

"It's amazing," said Izumi.

But, like a birthday candle being blown out, the smile faded from Grace's lips. "Now I have ruined everything," she sighed. "All these years later, because of me and my clumsiness, Scarlet has been taken back by the sea. She will have to stay there for the rest of her life."

"That's enough now. You need to rest," said Fairy Godmother Pom, taking Grace's empty hot-chocolate cup.

She tucked Izumi in too.

"Scarlet's parents are on their way. There is nothing we can do until they arrive," said Flintheart firmly.

 199

"We are all doing everything we can," said Lady DuLac.

"But that's just it," whispered Grace the moment the teachers shut the door and hurried away downstairs. "There is nothing anyone else can do. The only person who can save Scarlet is me."

CHAPTER TWENTY-TWO
The Locket

Grace leapt out of bed and began to pace round and round the tiny dormitory.

"The sea has taken Scarlet to pay my debt," she said as Izumi sat up. "Her parents won't be able to help no matter how many jewels they bring with them."

"You're right. The gift must be from you," agreed Izumi. "And it must be something that comes from the sea, otherwise the Returning Pool will just toss it back."

"Like the diamonds," sighed Grace, looking

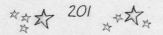

at the beautiful necklace lying on her bedside table. She still found it hard to believe it had not been enough to please the sea. Now she needed something even better — something that would stop poor Scarlet turning into to a mermaid like her great-grandmother Princess Turquoise had once been.

"Look!" Grace picked up the little silver locket Scarlet had laid carefully on her own bedside table before they had gone down to the sea. "I wish she had this with her. It might bring her luck — or at least make her feel better"

Both girls fell silent, thinking of their gentle friend and how frightened she must be.

"It's all my stupid fault!" said Grace crossly. She ran the silver chain of the locket through her fingers and began to fiddle with the catch.

"Careful," warned Izumi.

It was too late. "Whoa!" The locket

slipped from Grace's hand and fell to the floor with a terrible clattering sound.

As it hit the ground, the silver catch which had been stuck shut for so long sprang free with a *ping*!

"It's open," gasped Grace, scrabbling for the locket. "And there's something inside."

"Let's see!" Izumi jumped out of bed and stared over Grace's shoulder.

There were two tiny portraits inside the locket. Each was of a young girl wearing a Tall Towers uniform from long ago.

"That one is the spitting image of Scarlet," said Grace, pointing to the tiny picture in the right-hand side of the frame. It showed a smiling princess with long red hair.

"And that one looks just like you," laughed Izumi, pointing to the left-hand side where a wild-haired princess with freckles grinned out at them.

"Turquoise and Joy!" said Grace and Izumi at exactly the same time.

The princesses in the pictures were still smiling as brightly as if they had been painted yesterday.

"This must be a friendship locket," said Izumi.

Grace was staring closely at the tiny portraits. "Look!" she said, "My Great-Grandmother Joy is wearing the pearls – the same ones that Precious has now."

"So she is," said Izumi.

But Grace was already charging down the stairs. "I've got it! I know how I can save Scarlet," she cried.

CHAPTER TWENTY-THREE
Precious's Pearls

"Precious? Are you here?" Grace skidded through the door to Treasure Dorm and landed in a heap on the floor. But there was no sign of her cousin.

"Why do you want to find Precious?" asked Izumi, hurrying into the posh gold-curtained dormitory behind her. "She's not going to help save Scarlet, is she?"

"She has to," said Grace. "Don't you see? The pearls are the prefect gift. They don't belong to me – but they do belong to my

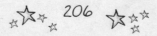

family, and they are of the sea."

"Of course," said Izumi. "Pearls come from the water. They are found inside oyster shells."

Grace glanced at the shiny gold clock on her cousin's golden dressing table. It was nine o'clock on Sunday morning. "Breakfast is over," she said. "Precious could be anywhere on the island by now." It was strange to think the other princesses would all be enjoying their free day, with no idea what had happened to Scarlet.

"Isn't this where the pearls are kept?" said Izumi, lifting a shell-shaped box from beside the clock.

"I think so. But they won't be in there," said Grace. "Precious never takes them off." She opened the lid but, just as she had expected, the shell-shaped box was empty.

"Look at that," said Izumi, pointing to an inscription inside the lid:

To Princess Joy
A gift from the sea.
Happy birthday!
From your very best friend,
Princess Turquoise.

"Goodness! So that's how the pearls came in to my family," said Grace. "Scarlet's Great-Grandmother Turquoise gave them to my Great-Grandmother Joy."

"They must be mermaid pearls," said Izumi.

"They'd be the perfect gift to save Scarlet," sighed Grace. "If only I could persuade Precious to give them away."

"Give what away?" asked Precious, barging through the door. "What are you doing in here, Grace? Lady DuLac just called us all to assembly and explained what terrible danger you have put poor Scarlet in."

"That's not what she said at all, Precious,"

tutted Visalotta, coming into the dormitory behind her. "But she did tell us everything that has happened. I hope Scarlet's all right. I wish there was something I could do to help."

"Precious is the one who can help us now," said Grace, smiling imploringly at her cousin. "You see, your pearls are the perfect gift to give to the sea. I know they could set Scarlet free."

"No way!" spat Precious. "You're not having them."

"Your Great-Grandmother Joy's pearls were a birthday present from Scarlet's great-grandmother. Her name was Turquoise," Izumi explained. "They were best friends." She picked up the shell-shaped box from Precious's dressing table and read the inscription aloud.

"So what?" Precious didn't even look surprised.

Grace's mouth dropped open. "You knew that already," she said. "You must have read that message hundreds of times!"

"Maybe," shrugged Precious. "But how was I supposed to know who Turquoise was?"

"That's true, I suppose," murmured Grace.

But Visalotta stepped forward. "You may not have known that Turquoise was Scarlet's great-grandmother until this morning, Precious," she said. "But I saw your face as soon as Lady DuLac mentioned her name in assembly. You looked furious."

"Really furious," agreed Latisha. Most of the First Years had now gathered in the doorway to hear what was going on. "I saw it too."

"You must have guessed that giving away the pearls was the right thing to do," said Izumi.

"Well, I'm not doing it," said Precious, stamping her foot. "Not for anyone!"

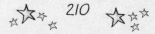

"Not even to save Scarlet?" begged Grace, shocked that Precious didn't seem to care about anything except keeping the necklace for herself.

"Why should I want to help Scarlet?" sneered Precious. "Everyone thinks she's so beautiful and perfect. She might be the best dancer in the class, but now we know she's not even a proper princess. She's part fish, for goodness' sake!"

A gasp of horror rose up from the First Year princesses. Even the twins looked shocked.

"That's a terrible thing to say," cried Visalotta.

"You take that back, Precious," said Grace.

"Why should I?" sneered Precious. "You got Scarlet into this mess. You should get her out of it."

"But I can't!" said Grace. "Not without a gift. It needs to be something of the sea that belongs to me and was freely given."

"Well, the pearls don't belong to you, do they," said Precious. "They belong to me. So there!"

"But Grace doesn't want them for herself," said Visalotta. "Can't you see that?"

"The pearls belong to our family," said Grace. "The sea might accept them. Joy was my great-grandmother too."

"You've already got her diamonds," snapped Precious. "You're not getting your grubby little paws on the pearls too."

"I'm not so sure about that," cried Grace. She flew out the door and thundered up the stairs again. "I have something that might just change your mind."

"And this isn't a trick?" Precious stared at Grace, her mouth wide open. "You are going to give me the diamonds? To keep? For

ever?" She whooped and spun around the room in a pirouette.

"Yes," said Grace. "If you'll swap them for the pearls."

"Deal!" Without even glancing at the pearls, Precious unclipped them from her neck and tossed them towards Grace. "Why would I keep those plain old things when I can have sparkly diamonds instead?"

"Here you are then." Grace handed over the diamonds. "I hope they'll make you happy, Precious," she said. Then she turned and walked out of the room as quickly as she could.

"That must have been so hard for you," said Izumi when they were alone in their own dormitory again. "Especially as the diamonds were from your mum."

"They were far too grand for me," smiled Grace. "Mama wouldn't mind. Not if it meant I could save Scarlet." She picked up the faded label which had been tied to the diamonds when she first unwrapped them on her birthday. "Giving is a far greater gift than receiving," she read. "I know now what Mama meant."

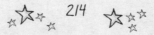

CHAPTER TWENTY-FOUR
Return to Mermaid Rock

As night fell, Grace and Izumi waited on the beach with Lady DuLac and Fairy Godmother Flint. Scarlet's parents were there. Her mother had the same sea-green eyes as Scarlet, flashing bright with worry as she stared out at the sea. Her father paced up and down the sand, almost colliding with Grace who was pacing too.

"Look," Grace cried as Waverley's head bobbed above the waves at last, and she swam to the shore to meet them. The

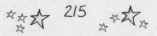

young mermaid seemed fully recovered, her sparkling silver tail shimmering in the light of the full moon.

"I wanted to be the one to take you back to Mermaid Rock," she said. "I've left Scarlet with the queen and Oceana. She is being very brave."

"But how will we call the dolphins?" said Grace, desperate to get going. "Scarlet sang for them last time."

"Shall I try?" said Scarlet's mother. She stepped forward and sang — in the same strange beautiful voice that Scarlet had used. Almost at once, two dolphins swam to the shore. "Bring Scarlet back safely," said her mother, biting her lip just as her daughter always did.

"I will, I promise," said Grace.

"Thank you!" Scarlet's father bowed to Grace and Izumi in turn.

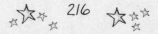

"We will wait here on the beach for you," said Lady DuLac. It had already been agreed that the solemn ceremony would be best if the two girls visited the mermaids alone.

"Have you got the pearls?" Izumi checked as they clambered on to the slippery dolphins.

"Of course," smiled Grace. "Even I am not that hopeless." She touched the necklace, which was clipped tightly around her neck. "I just hope this works." She knew the pearls came from the sea, but the gift was also supposed to be something that had been given freely and with love.

"Precious had to be forced to give up the pearls," she called to Izumi as they followed Waverley and rode their dolphins side by side across the waves. "And she doesn't feel any love for me – or for Scarlet – that's for sure."

"But she does love those shiny diamonds,"

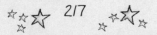

hollered Izumi. "She gave the pearls quite freely as soon as she saw those."

"You're right," Grace smiled. She felt a fresh surge of hope and hugged her dolphin so tightly that it leapt out of the water in surprise.

Scarlet was still standing in the middle of the pool when the girls reached the grotto. Her face lit up as she saw Grace and Izumi. "I knew you'd come," she cried.

The ring of silver light around her was so bright that Grace could not see her legs any more.

"We must be quick," said the queen.

Grace unclipped the pearls from around her neck and stepped to the edge of the Returning Pool.

"Wait. You'll need this," said Oceana, handing Grace the scroll to read from.

But Grace shook her head. She remembered the words perfectly:

I give thanks, kind mermaid, for saving me

Grace glanced over her shoulder and smiled at Waverley.

And offer this gift to repay the sea
Given freely with love, this treasure
  once mine
Shall return to the sea till the end
  of time.

Then, taking great care, Grace slipped the pearls gently into the water.

A faint ripple stirred the surface.

"Can you move yet?" asked Grace. But Scarlet shook her head.

Grace stared at the water, holding her

breath, barely daring to breathe.

Nothing happened.

"This is hopeless," she groaned. But slowly – very slowly – the silver light began to fade. The water was turning blue and clear once more.

Scarlet stumbled forward.

She's free!" cheered Grace.

"Quick," cried the queen, motioning to Grace and Izumi. "Run into the water and save her. We cannot help or it will break the mermaid code again. But Scarlet is far too weak to swim to safety. She will no longer have her mermaid powers now."

Grace and Izumi splashed into the pool without waiting to be asked twice. They grabbed Scarlet's arms and pulled her to safety.

She lay on the polished floor between them and rolled herself into a ball, her long legs pulled up underneath her chin. "Thank you!" she smiled.

Suddenly, the waters of the Returning Pool began to swirl and churn again.

"Oh goodness! It's not going to throw the pearls out, is it?" asked Grace.

"I don't think so," said Waverley.

But a fountain rose up in the middle of the water and Grace saw the pearl necklace flung into the air just as the diamonds had been.

"But the pearls are of the sea," she cried. "Why doesn't the water want to keep them?"

"Watch," said the Mermaid Queen as Grace saw the string break from the pearls and each white bead drop back into the water. Peering down, she saw that the pearls had formed a bright mosaic on the bottom of the pool.

"How beautiful," said Izumi.

Grace helped Scarlet to her feet and they all stared down at the shining design – a perfect full moon made of pearls.

"It is over!" Waverley dived into the water and leapt up high like a dolphin. "Thank you!" she cheered.

The queen and the other mermaids clapped.

Izumi, Scarlet and Grace all hugged each other. Grace was glad her cheeks were still wet with salty water from the pool so that nobody could see she was crying. With the help of Izumi, she had saved a young mermaid and her best friend too.

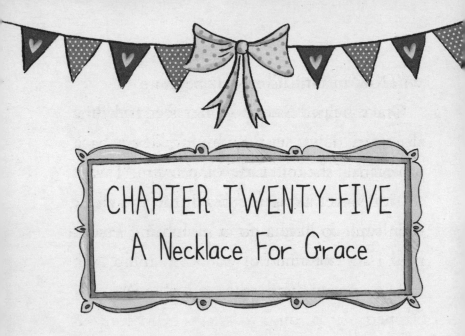

CHAPTER TWENTY-FIVE
A Necklace For Grace

After Scarlet's parents had gone home, she was ordered to spend a whole week in bed to make sure she was fully recovered. Fairy Godmother Pom made a dreadful fuss of her, and Grace and Izumi spent all their free time in the dormitory. The other princesses in the class visited often too. They drew get-well cards for Scarlet and brought her treats and books. Visalotta even gave her a beautiful gold music box with a silver, spinning ballerina inside so that she could

wind it up and listen to the tune.

The shy princess was embarrassed by all the attention. "I just wish things would get back to normal," she told Grace and Izumi. "I want to ride Velvet along the beach for a picnic. I even want to have a go at swimming lessons now. I am not afraid of water any more. Not now I know I have mermaid blood."

"Waverley's going to start a synchronized swimming team," said Grace. "She plans to organize a water dance display for the Summer Open Day at the end of term. She wants you to be captain."

"Me?" Scarlet blushed.

"Synchronized swimming's a bit like ballet in water," said Izumi. "You'll be brilliant."

"I don't think Waverley is going to want *me* for the team," laughed Grace. "I'd only swim left when everybody else was swimming right! But I've persuaded her to

have a competition after the show to see who can make the biggest splash when they dive-bomb off the rocks. I might have a chance of winning that."

Scarlet and Izumi giggled. Even though they were Grace's very best friends, they had to agree she'd be much better at dive-bombing than taking part in a synchronized-swimming routine.

"I hope the display goes well for Waverley," said Grace. "It's the last time she'll be teaching at Tall Towers. She's going to start training properly for the Seven Oceans Endurance Race after that."

"And good riddance to her," said Precious, poking her head around the dormitory door. She had finally come to visit, even though it was Scarlet's last day in bed. "I didn't bring you a get-well card, as I see you are better already," she said. "But I do

want to say thank you."

"Thank you?" said Scarlet. "What for?"

"Without your little adventures, I would never have got to keep these beautiful diamonds," said Precious, stretching her neck and sticking her nose in the air. "They suit me so much better than Grace."

Izumi and Scarlet rolled their eyes. Precious looked ridiculous, strutting around in front of the mirror like a peacock.

Grace collapsed in giggles as Precious finally stopped showing off and flounced out of the room. "It's not fair, Scarlet," she groaned. "Why do you get to have a distant cousin who is a beautiful mermaid like Waverley? And I get to have Cousin Precious instead!"

"It must be dreadful to see her parading about like that," said Scarlet. "Do you miss the diamonds terribly?"

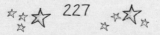

"Not really," said Grace truthfully. "Precious is right. They really were far too fancy for me. I'd be frightened to wear them. They'd be sure to fly off if I was galloping Billy along the beach."

"But you didn't get to keep the pearls either," said Scarlet, clutching her beloved silver locket, which had been mended and was hanging around her neck once again. "That means you don't have a necklace at all."

"I have been thinking about that," said Grace. She slid across the floor in her big, fluffy, yak-hair slippers and opened the drawer beside her bed.

She ran her fingers gently across the faded birthday note from Mama and smiled to herself as she remembered the wise words which had shown her that giving the diamonds away was the right thing to do. She had found their true worth at last. Then

she lifted up a little blue box which was tucked away in the back of the drawer.

She took out the homemade shell necklace that her two best friends had given her and tied the ribbon around her neck.

"There!" she said, with a big grin. "How could I ever ask for anything more valuable than that?"

It's Grace's first term at Tall Towers Princess Academy and she can't wait to make friends, meet her unicorn and learn how to be the perfect princess. If only Grace wasn't the clumsiest pupil that Tall Towers has ever had. . . Can she prove that being a princess is about more than being perfect?

Princess DisGrace

DisGrace

First Term
at Tall Towers

Lou Kuenzler

Spring is in the air – and the princesses must perform in the Ballet of the Flowers. If only Grace wasn't so clumsy! But she has other things on her mind – a row with her friends, a mysterious baby unicorn, and rumours that the dragons on Coronet Island aren't extinct after all. . .

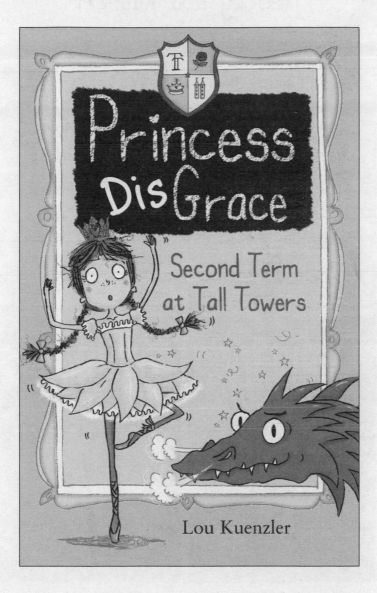

Princess DisGrace

Second Term at Tall Towers

Lou Kuenzler

Also by Lou Kuenzler

LOU KUENZLER
SHRINKING VIOLET
NORMAL size one minute, FISH FINGER-size the next!
ACTUAL SIZE!

LOU KUENZLER
SHRINKING VIOLET
DEFINITELY NEEDS A DOG
ACTUAL SIZE!
NORMAL size one minute, DOG BISCUIT-size the next!

LOU KUENZLER
SHRINKING VIOLET
IS TOTALLY FAMOUS
ACTUAL SIZE!
NORMAL size one minute, LIPSTICK-size the next!

LOU KUENZLER
SHRINKING VIOLET
ABSOLUTELY LOVES ANCIENT EGYPT
NORMAL size one minute, MINIATURE-size the next!